Y0-BEM-992

God's Workmanship Under Grace

Exploring the Believer's Blessings In Christ

Thomas Edward Bertoli

To my friends Wayne and Joan
God bless you
Tommy

ACW Press
ACW Press
Ozark, AL 36360

Except where otherwise indicated all Scripture quotations are taken from the New American Standard Bible®, Copyright © 1960, 1962, 1963, 1968, 1971, 1972, 1973, 1975, 1977, 1995 by The Lockman Foundation. Used by permission.

Verses marked NIV are taken from the Holy Bible, New International Version®. Copyright © 1973, 1978, 1984 by the International Bible Society. Used by permission of Zondervan Publishing House. The "NIV" and "New International Version" trademarks are registered in the United States Patent and Trademark Office by International Bible Society.

Verses marked TLB are taken from The Living Bible, Copyright © 1971 owned by assignment by Illinois Regional Bank N.A. (As trustee). Used by permission of Tyndale House Publishers, Inc., Wheaton, Illinois 60189. All rights reserved.

God's Workmanship Under Grace
Copyright ©2005 Tom Bertoli
All rights reserved

Cover Design by Alpha Advertising
Cover Photo: Pine Hill Graphics
Interior Design by Pine Hill Graphics

Packaged by ACW Press
85334 Lorane Hwy
Eugene, Oregon 97405
www.acwpress.com
The views expressed or implied in this work do not necessarily reflect those of ACW Press. Ultimate design, content, and editorial accuracy of this work is the responsibility of the author(s).

Library of Congress Cataloging-in-Publication Data
(Provided by Cassidy Cataloguing Services, Inc.)

Bertoli, Thomas Edward.

    God's workmanship under grace : exploring the believer's
    blessings in Christ / Thomas Edward Bertoli. — 1st ed. — Ozark, AL :
    ACW Press, 2005.

        p. ; cm.
        ISBN: 1-932124-38-1

    1. Christian life. 2. Spirituality. 3. Spiritual life. I. Title.

BV4501.3 .B47 2005
248.4—dc22   0503

All rights reserved. No part of this book may be reproduced, stored in a retrieval system, or transmitted in any form or by any means—electronic, mechanical, photocopying, recording, or otherwise—without prior permission in writing from the copyright holder except as provided by USA copyright law.

Printed in the United States of America.

Dedication

This book is dedicated to Pastor John Michaels of Calvary Chapel Spring Valley, Las Vegas, Nevada. Since the inception of the church in 1986, his faithfulness to his calling has stood the test of time. Through his leadership, countless blessings have poured out of the church, in which the lives of many have been touched by the grace of God. I personally want to thank Pastor John for his love and kindness in bringing me aboard in 1997, and providing the many opportunities to pursue the path and direction that God has placed upon my life. He will always have a special place in my heart.

Acknowledgments

I would like to thank, with much appreciation, my good friends Isam Itson, Brown Suffield, Yaser Makram, and Tim Matthias for their kindness and time in reviewing my manuscripts. Their comments and friendships were of enormous value to me in the writing process of this book.

In addition, special thanks to my wife, Marie, who has always been there to encourage me in reaching the desires and goals that God has set before me in serving Him.

Contents

Prologue

O come, let us sing for joy to the LORD,
Let us shout joyfully to the rock of our salvation.
Let us come before His presence with thanksgiving,
Let us shout joyfully to Him with psalms.
For the LORD is a great God
And a great King above all gods,
In whose hand are the depths of the earth,
The peaks of the mountains are His also.
The sea is His, for it was He who made it,
And His hands formed the dry land.
Come, let us worship and bow down,
Let us kneel before the LORD our Maker.
For He is our God,
And we are the people of His pasture and the sheep of His hand.
(Psalm 95:1-7a)

The psalmist is worshipping God as he reflects on the majestic ways of the Lord. He speaks of God's wonder in creation and His sovereignty over all things. His intimate relationship with God in his personal life is what prompts him to worship in this worthy manner.

Revival in a believer's heart begins when he understands the greatness of God in all His ways. Those who have walked with God through faith and have trusted in His Word in their daily lives have tasted the goodness and wonderful blessings that accompany salvation. As the New Testament believer grows in the

Lord he becomes fully aware of all his blessings in Christ—utilizing them in order to persevere in the faith through the hardships and tribulations of life.

The most powerful weapon that Satan uses against the believer is creating doubt in his mind. The devil is constantly trying to misrepresent God's love for His people and, in so doing, blinds them from seeing the reality of their blessings in Jesus Christ. When Satan has accomplished this, he has destroyed the believer's hope in God, crippling the believer emotionally, and taking away any drive to walk in the fullness of the faith. The believer can guard against this by cultivating his relationship with God on a daily basis. In this way he will witness the abundant grace he has in Jesus Christ and realize the awesome power available to him in fighting back against the schemes of Satan.

This book explores all the wonderful blessings that have become the possession of every member in the body of Christ, the church. The believer will witness the treasures of God's kindness to those who love Him. In so doing, I hope that God's people will be encouraged and reflect the purpose of their calling, to glorify God in every aspect of the Christian faith.

Therefore humble yourselves under the mighty hand of God, that He may exalt you at the proper time, **casting all your anxiety on Him, because He cares for you.** (1 Peter 5:6-7, emphasis added)

Chapter One

THE
GOSPEL

As to this salvation, the prophets who prophesied of the grace that would come to you made careful searches and inquiries, seeking to know what person or time the Spirit of Christ within them was indicating as He predicted the sufferings of Christ and the glories to follow. It was revealed to them that they were not serving themselves, but you, in these things which now have been announced to you through those who preached the gospel to you by the Holy Spirit sent from heaven—things into which angels long to look. Therefore, prepare your minds for action, keep sober in spirit, fix your hope completely on the grace to be brought to you at the revelation of Jesus Christ. (1 Peter 1:10-13)

There are many riches in this world that man is striving to attain in order to find fulfillment, but none is more precious or valuable than the treasures of the gospel message, which provides everything necessary for the well-being of man. The gospel contains the way and riches of salvation that are the property of God's people who believe in Him.

The passage above relates how the Old Testament prophets anxiously looked into this future time when the Messiah would come and open the door to the floodgates of God's grace. That time had arrived in the first coming of Jesus Christ. The believer is encouraged to prepare his mind once and for all, taking to heart the present reality of this fulfilled prophecy, with all the wonderful blessings that accompany its fulfillment.

In its broadest sense, the word *gospel* means good news or good tidings of the kingdom of God. The usage of the word *gospel* in this chapter emphasizes the essence of the message as it relates to the sacrifice of Jesus Christ and all its benefits to those who believe. That is, Christ took on humanity, He died for our sins, He rose from the dead, and everyone who puts faith in Him will be forgiven for their sins. They will partake of God's grace and blessings for all eternity. This is the heart of the gospel message.

> *For I delivered to you as of first importance what I also received, that Christ died for our sins according to the Scriptures, and that He was buried, and that He was raised on the third day according to the Scriptures.*
> (1 Corinthians 15:3-4)

> *For the Scripture says, "WHOEVER BELIEVES IN HIM WILL NOT BE DISAPPOINTED." For there is no distinction between Jew and Greek; for the same* Lord *is Lord of all, abounding in riches for all who call on Him; for WHOEVER WILL CALL ON THE NAME OF THE LORD WILL BE SAVED."* (Romans 10:11-13)

THE IMPORTANCE OF THE GOSPEL

The unquestionable importance of the gospel is given in Romans 1:16-17.

For I am not ashamed of the gospel, for it is the power of God for salvation to everyone who believes, to the Jew first and also to the Greek. For in it the righteousness of God is revealed from faith to faith; as it is written, "BUT THE RIGHTEOUS Man SHALL LIVE BY FAITH." (Romans 1:16-17)

Reflecting on this passage, certain issues demand our attention. First, *Paul is not ashamed to identify with the gospel message.* He was not ashamed because he understood the present and eternal value of the gospel for man. It is sad to note how people have continued to pursue earthly treasures that throughout the ages have failed to satisfy the emptiness that is in all of us. Man is proud to identify himself with fame, money, and material things that leave him unfulfilled, yet is ashamed to identify himself with Christ who is the only one who can bring satisfaction and fulfillment in this life. Paul identified with Christ because he knew that in Him was the embodiment of all truth and the blessings that come to those who believe in Him.

Second, *the nature of the gospel has a power that far outweighs anything in this world.* When one thinks of power he is inclined to describe it in many ways. For instance, power is the ability to lift five hundred pounds in a weight-lifting event, or the engine of a jumbo jet that can lift that huge craft off the ground, or even the power of a nuclear warhead that can wipe out a whole city. That's power. But the power of the gospel message is of a different nature, and far more potent than all the powers in the world put together. *The power of the gospel imparts eternal life to man.* It provides man with victory over death. The thought that man can conquer death provides the necessary hope in which his soul finds rest and overcomes the weariness of everyday life.

The third thing that comes to us in this passage is the *scope of the gospel.* The gospel is for everyone and is the only road that leads to heaven. Those who insist on promoting many ways to heaven apart from Christ are challenging the divine truth of God's Word for salvation. Jesus said, *I am the way, and the truth and the life; No one comes to the Father but through Me* (John 14:6). He is the only way to the Father. He is the truth, in which His person and word reveal the very will of the Father, and in Him is eternal life. Those who pursue another means of salvation or reject the truth of Christ will fail to enter into the eternal blessings of God that are revealed in the gospel message.

Fourth, *faith in Christ alone is the means by which one receives salvation and partakes of all the wonderful blessings of the gospel.* For those who have put faith in Christ, the power and penalty of sin that separate man from God (see below) have been disarmed. Believers escape God's wrath toward sin and are beneficiaries of all God's blessings promised to those who believe in Jesus Christ. Those benefits include the righteousness of Christ, the standard of holiness for the church saint, *which is imputed* to the believer through faith. That is, the believer is declared holy and perfect before God because of Christ in him, and is equipped with all the resources necessary to walk according to the righteousness of God. The promised Holy Spirit, who has taken up residence in every believer's life, sanctifies him on a daily basis (see chapter 4), enabling him to live in his new standing in Christ.

THE NECESSITY FOR THE GOSPEL

In order to understand the necessity for the gospel, one needs to understand the biblical concept of sin and the meaning of salvation. *Salvation in its purest sense is deliverance from the power and penalty of sin.* The sin issue has to be dealt with in order to bring restoration to man. The true nature of sin and how it relates to man cannot be limited to an act of disobedience as most people define it, but goes far beyond this general understanding. Man is defenseless when doing battle with sin. It is not within the makeup of man to overcome the sin that dominates his character. In fact, his whole makeup is bent on sin. The biblical term that best defines sin's essence is *sinful nature*, a nature that is disobedient or in rebellion against God, which everyone is born with since the fall of Adam. All men have sinned; therefore, all fall under the penalty of sin (*For the wages of sin is death,* Romans 6:23a).

> *Therefore, just as through one man sin entered into the world, and death through sin, and so death spread to all men, because all sinned.* (Romans 5:12)

An individual commits acts of sin because it is his nature (the sinful or fallen nature) and therefore he is only reacting and living out who he truly is. The good news is that God understands this and has provided a means by which man may overcome this deficiency, which if not remedied will not only keep him separated from God's blessings in the present but for all eternity. The remedy is in Christ, because *Christ is the only one who can bridge the gap of sin* that separates man from God.

THE BELIEVER IS GOD'S WORKMANSHIP

Through faith, the believer becomes the workmanship of God created in Christ Jesus for good works:

> *For we are His workmanship, created in Christ Jesus for good works, which God prepared beforehand so that we would walk in them.* (Ephesians 2:10)

This Scripture is the basis for writing this book. It is like a capsule that contains all the theological truths of the believer who is saved by faith in Jesus Christ. The word *workmanship* is the key to this verse. It denotes, "a work of art or a masterpiece."[1] The believer is God's masterpiece created in Christ Jesus in order to produce the fruits of righteousness, testifying to the truth of God's Word as His ambassador on earth. The present tense of the verb, "we *are* his workmanship" emphasizes the *positional truth* (our new standing before God) of the believer, when he is saved by faith at conversion. As God's children, the Father sees us as perfect in Christ, a beautiful work of art.

God is displaying us to mankind as His masterpiece, therefore we are to walk according to our calling in obedience and humility and produce the fruit of righteousness. This calling in the believer's life shows the awesome responsibility and privilege placed upon every believer to uphold the truth.

GOD'S PURPOSE IN THE BELIEVER'S CALLING

God has chosen sinful man who has called upon Him for forgiveness as His ambassadors and instruments to reveal and witness to the righteousness of Jesus Christ and His teachings. God has not chosen the heroes of this world or men who are considered great from a worldly perspective to uphold His cause. He has chosen those who recognize the testimony of Christ and have put their faith in Him. Many of the rich and famous who reject the testimony of Christ are the heroes of this world. Those who believe God are *the heroes of heaven*. The author of Hebrews, addressing the issue of faith, commends the Old Testament saints because they believed God (Hebrews 11:2). They were despised by man and considered fools, but were precious in the eyes of

---

1. John F. Walvoord, Roy B. Zuck, *The Bible Knowledge Commentary* (USA, Victor Books 1987), page 624

God. The exercise of their faith was considered more valuable to God than any treasures of this life (cf. 1 Peter 1:7). The believer is encouraged to follow in the same footsteps of these great men of faith (cf. Hebrews 12:1-3).

We, who have put faith in Christ, are those chosen instruments to be holy and blameless for all eternity. We are the light of the world that shines upon the darkness that has overtaken man's heart, bringing a message of hope to those in despair. We are the instruments that chip away at the hardness of people's hearts, helping them to understand the gospel, and enabling them to enter into the blessings of God through faith. God has chosen the simple people of this world, who have put faith in Him, to shame the wise.

> *For consider your calling, brethren, that there were not many wise according to the flesh, not many mighty, not many noble; but God has chosen the foolish things of the world to shame the wise, and God has chosen the weak things of the world to shame the things which are strong, and the base things of the world and the despised God has chosen, the things that are not, so that He may nullify the things that are, so that no man may boast before God. But by His doing you are in Christ Jesus, who became to us wisdom from God, and righteousness and sanctification, and redemption, so that, just as it is written, "LET HIM WHO BOASTS, BOAST IN THE LORD."* (1 Corinthians 1:26-31)

THE DIVINE POWER OF THE GOSPEL

The Apostle Peter in his second epistle testifies to the divine power of the gospel. God has not left us without the resources to fulfill our role.

*To those who have received a faith of the same kind as
ours, by the righteousness of our God and Savior, Jesus
Christ: Grace and peace be multiplied to you in the knowledge of God and of Jesus our Lord;* **seeing that His divine
power has granted to us everything pertaining to life
and godliness,** *through the true knowledge of Him who
called us by His own glory and excellence. For by these He
has granted to us His precious and magnificent promises,*
**so that by them you may become partakers of the
divine nature,** *having escaped the corruption that is in the
world by lust.* (2 Peter 1:1b-4, emphasis added)

The believer is partaking of the divine nature of God through
the Holy Spirit; therefore, he is able to walk in the things pertaining to godliness.

THE CALL TO COURAGE

The world system is diabolically opposed to the people of God.
It takes men and women of courage to persevere through this life as
children of God. Contrary to what many believe about Christians,
the message of the Bible is not for wimps, but for men and women
who have character and integrity, people of courage who have been
built up in their faith. The words of God when He commissioned
Joshua, "Be strong and courageous" (Joshua 1:9), are once again
being echoed in the hearts of New Testament believers.

*Be on the alert, stand firm in the faith, act like men, be strong.
Let all that you do be done in love.* (1 Corinthians 16:13-14)

The above passage adds the admonishment of doing everything in love. The church saint must balance his firm stance and

courage against the world system with the love of Jesus Christ. He is to press on with God's grace and love, standing firm in the faith against all opposition to the gospel message. The mature Christian knows how to delve into the resources made available to him in Christ; therefore, he is able to persevere in all the fullness of truth and love.

THE BELIEVER'S PURPOSE

It is of utmost importance that the believer understands why he is a Christian and what his obligation is before God. He is God's chosen instrument to be holy and blameless, penetrating the darkness that covers the hearts of men.

Do all things without grumbling or disputing; so that you will prove yourselves to be blameless and innocent, children of God above reproach in the midst of a crooked and perverse generation, among whom you appear as lights in the world, holding fast the word of life. (Philippians 2:14-16a)

The believer who has been purified and sanctified in Christ is obligated to live according to his new calling in Christ, fulfilling his purpose as a holy instrument of God. Many Christians today fail to recognize this reality to their calling in Christ. They are defeated or complacent because of their failure to understand their divine purpose. Without a proper perspective, the believer will fail to live in the fullness of the Christian faith. He will fail to live a Spirit-filled life (see chapter 7), which is to pursue holiness and righteousness in his obligation to God. Anything short of this obligation diminishes a believer's value in the body of Christ.

This book testifies to the storehouse of riches that God has made available to us to complete our mission. Are we up to the task to commit our lives to our calling and stand firm as God's witnesses to a dying world that has turned its back on God? With this in mind let us now explore the wonderful blessings we possess through God's grace, which has been poured out on us abundantly through Jesus Christ.

Chapter Two

THE HEAVENLY CALLING
OF THE BELIEVER

For this reason I too, having heard of the faith in the Lord Jesus which exists among you and your love for all the saints, do not cease giving thanks for you, while making mention of you in my prayers; that the God of our Lord Jesus Christ, the Father of glory, may give to you a spirit of wisdom and of revelation in the knowledge of Him. I pray that the eyes of your heart may be enlightened, so that you will know what is the hope of His calling, what are the riches of the glory of His inheritance in the saints, and what is the surpassing greatness of His power toward us who believe. These are in accordance with the working of the strength of His might which He brought about in Christ, when He raised Him from the dead and seated Him at His right hand in the heavenly places, far above all rule and authority and power and dominion, and every name that is named, not only in this age but also in the one to come. (Ephesians 1:15-21)

This prayer by the Apostle Paul comes at the conclusion of the heavenly calling of the believer, which he addressed in chapter one of Ephesians. He begins his prayer with the words "For this reason," which directs the believer back to what he has previously said. He had just revealed to the saints, (God's masterpieces) all the magnificent blessings bestowed upon them through their faith in Jesus Christ. He wants his fellow brothers and sisters in the Lord to thoroughly understand the eternal riches they have in Christ; therefore, he prays that they capture these eternal truths and take to heart the things that are truly meaningful to their personal lives in Christ.

Examining Ephesians 1:3-14, we will see why Paul was prompted to pray in such a manner. Doing so, we as God's people will be enlightened and encouraged to see God's plan in our heavenly calling. All three persons of the Godhead—the Father, the Son, and the Holy Spirit—are involved in this eternal calling of the believer.

THE ROLE OF THE FATHER

The role of the Father is revealed to us in Ephesians 1:3-6:

Blessed be the God and Father of our Lord Jesus Christ, who has blessed us with every spiritual blessing in the heavenly places in Christ, just as He chose us in Him before the foundation of the world, that we would be holy and blameless before Him. In love He predestined us to adoption as sons through Jesus Christ to Himself, according to the kind intention of His will, to the praise of the glory of His grace, which He freely bestowed on us in the Beloved.

Blessed with Every Spiritual Blessing

In verse 3, the Father has blessed us with every spiritual blessing in the heavenly places in Christ. When the Father blesses us it is not merely a good feeling we experience, but an equipping in our lives that enables us to walk in the fullness of joy, peace, and righteousness provided in the believer's calling. These blessings of God bestowed on us go far beyond any blessings we can comprehend in this life (*"spiritual blessings in the heavenly places"*). They are blessings that edify and restore the believer to a proper relationship to God for all eternity. They far outweigh the material riches of this world, which are here today and gone tomorrow. The temporary nature of earthly blessings fades in comparison to the eternal blessings that God has bestowed on us. The sphere of these blessings is in the person of Jesus Christ. *Only in Him* do we have access to these wonderful blessings provided by the Father. Those who have never repented from their sins are outside this realm and remain in a state of unrighteousness.

Chosen before Creation

In verse 4, we see the origin and nature of these heavenly blessings. The Father chose us before the foundations of the world in our heavenly calling. This election by God in His sovereignty was an expression of the Father's unending love and grace to us who believe. We were the apple of His eye before we ever took our first breath. The purpose of our election was to be *holy and blameless* for all eternity. The word *holy* emphasizes the fact that we, in our new union with Christ, have been set apart from the evil of this world and dedicated to the worship and service of God. The word *saint* comes from the word *holy*. Biblically speaking, anyone who is in Christ is a saint set apart for the work of God. Being blameless literally means "without blemish, free from any fault." The term was used of a sacrificial animal in the Old Testament that was without any flaws and was acceptable before God (cf. Leviticus 1:3,10; 3:1). In the same way, we appear to God as His holy instruments, without blemish because of what Christ has done for us on the cross. This new standing and acceptance by God is everlasting.

Predestined as God's Adopted Children

In love (verse 5), the Father predestined to adopt us as His own children according to the good pleasure of His will. The word *predestined* means to be marked out beforehand. When referring to the calling of the believer, it means his destiny is determined before birth. Before we were born, God had already purposed to adopt us as His children, and to bestow all these eternal blessings on us. The implications of our adoption by God should not be missed. In Roman times, an adopted son was brought into the family and given the same rights and privileges of a child who was born naturally into the family. He was entitled to the inheritance as an heir to the family fortune. In the same way, we, as God's children are heirs along with Christ of the eternal inheritance that is waiting for those who have put faith in Him.

> *The Spirit Himself testifies with our spirit that we are children of God, and if children, heirs also, heirs of God and fellow heirs with Christ, if indeed we suffer with Him so that we may also be glorified with Him.* (Romans 8:16-17)

> *Because you are sons, God has sent forth the Spirit of His Son into our hearts, crying, "Abba! Father!" Therefore you are no longer a slave, but a son; and if a son, then an heir through God.* (Galatians 4:6-7)

This awesome privilege as children of God is a reflection of His great love for us.

> *How great is the love the Father has lavished on us, that we should be called children of God! And that is what we are!* (I John 3:1a NIV)

The Father's Delight in the Believer's Calling

All this was according to God's good pleasure and His perfect will (Ephesians 1:5). God was delighted to impart His spiritual blessings and riches to His children. His perfect will is rooted in the essence of His person, which is love (cf. 1 John 4:8). We, who have put faith in Jesus Christ, are the recipients of the endless love of God. The believer needs to understand the depths of God's love, which is characterized by mercy and grace. It is a powerful motive compelling the saints to serve God with all of their hearts. The Apostle Paul was driven by God's love for him through Christ, compelling him to pursue the Father's will with every part of his being.

> *For Christ's love compels us, because we are convinced that one died for all, and therefore all died.* (2 Corinthians 5:14 NIV)

The believer, who fully comprehends the love of the Father and the calling God has placed upon his life, will look to God in times of trouble. Many Christians do the same thing that Adam and Eve did when they committed the first sin of man, they hid from God (Genesis 3:8). God wants His children, who are struggling, not to hide from Him but to run to Him, in order to receive mercy and grace, which are necessary in persevering through the hardships and tribulations of this life. God loves His people. Make that love relationship complete by walking in the fullness of our Christian faith.

THE ROLE OF THE SON

The role of the Son in our heavenly calling is recorded for us in verses 7-12 of the passage.

In Him we have redemption through His blood, the for-giveness of our trespasses, according to the riches of His grace which He lavished on us. In all wisdom and insight He made known to us the mystery of His will, according to His kind intention which He purposed in Him with a view to an administration suitable to the fullness of the times, that is, the summing up of all things in Christ, things in the heavens and things on the earth. In Him also we have obtained an inheritance, having been predestined according to His purpose who works all things after the counsel of His will, to the end that we who were the first to hope in Christ would be to the praise of His glory. (Ephesians 1:7-12)

Redemption

In Christ, we have redemption through His blood and the forgiveness of our sins (Ephesians 1:7). The word *redemption* means to purchase or buy something. It was used of the purchasing of a slave *with the idea that he would gain his freedom in the transaction.* When it is used of believers, it indicates the release or deliverance from a state of punishment or slavery by the paying of a price. Three things are true of the believer when he is redeemed:

(1) He is delivered from the punishment or curse of the Law (Galatians 3:13; 4:5). The sacrifice of Christ redeemed the believer from the condemnation of the Law.

Christ redeemed us from the curse of the law by becoming a curse for us, for it is written: "Cursed is everyone who is hung on a tree." He redeemed us in order that the blessing given to Abraham might come to the Gentiles through Christ Jesus, so that by faith we might receive the promise of the Spirit. (Galatians 3:13-14 NIV)

(2) He is freed from the slavery of sin (Titus 2:14). Through redemption the believer is no longer under the power of sin.

> *...who gave himself for us to redeem us from all wicked-*
> *ness and to purify for himself a people that are his very*
> *own, eager to do what is good.* (Titus 2:14 NIV)

(3) The price of our redemption was paid for by the blood of Jesus Christ (1 Corinthians 6:20; Revelation 5:9; 1 Peter 1:18-19). The cost of redemption was high.

> *Knowing that you were not redeemed with perishable things*
> *like silver or gold from your futile way of life inherited from*
> *your forefathers, but with precious blood, as of a lamb*
> *unblemished and spotless, the blood of Christ.* (1 Peter 1:18-19)

God loved us so much that He redeemed us from the penalty and bondage of sin with the precious blood of His only begotten Son, Jesus Christ. This alone is a statement of God's unending love for those who believe.

Forgiveness

Forgiveness means the believer is pardoned from his sins forever. God refrains from inflicting the punishment that is due the believer (cf. Romans 5:9) that was divinely imposed (Romans 6:23). There is a complete removal of sin that separated the believer from God. The sin that was an insurmountable debt to overcome was erased by God's grace and mercy. One simple act of genuine faith by the believer in the atoning work of Jesus Christ at the cross is all that is required. King David, understanding the nature and depth of God's forgiveness through faith, cried out in these words:

What happiness for those whose guilt has been forgiven!
What joys when sins are covered over! What relief for
those who have confessed their sins and God has cleared
their record. (Psalm 32:1-2 TLB)

The Apostle Paul interjected these words in Romans 4 to show believers that forgiveness comes through faith and not through the Law (Galatians 3:12). The Law was good and had a purpose (cf. Galatians 3:24), but the Law could not save (Galatians 2:20-21). Only when one calls upon the Lord in faith will he be forgiven for his sin. How sad it is for those who think they need to earn God's forgiveness through their own personal works. King David was blessed because he understood the nature of God's grace working in those who come to God in faith.

Enlightened with All Spiritual Truth

In Ephesians 1:8-10, the believer in Christ has been enlightened with all spiritual truth. He is provided with *wisdom and insight* through Christ that reveal the Father's perfect will. Wisdom is the means by which the believer understands the ways of God. Insight applies this understanding to everyday life. The benefit of this is that we who are in Christ can comprehend the depths of God's Word and walk according to that knowledge. Paul in addressing the Colossians talks about Christ in this manner to the believers:

...and for all those who have not personally seen my face,
that their hearts may be encouraged, having been knit
together in love, and attaining to all the wealth that comes
from the full assurance of understanding, resulting in a
true knowledge of God's mystery, **that is, Christ Himself,**
in whom are hidden all the treasures of wisdom and
knowledge. (Colossians 2:1b, emphasis added)

To know Jesus Christ is to know God. If there are any secrets about God, they are all revealed in Jesus Christ. The believer through Christ knows the will of the Father. In the gospel period, Jesus encouraged the disciples, calling them friends and not slaves, because of the intimate relationship they had with the Father through Him.

No longer do I call you slaves, for the slave does not know what his master is doing; but I have called you friends, for all things that I have heard from My Father I have made known to you. (John 15:15)

As believers, we are no longer strangers to the ways of God and can now understand the depths of God's holiness and righteousness.

This intimacy we have with God should not go unnoticed. God is a father to His children whom He dearly loves and not a distant power who cannot identify with our daily needs. He is concerned about every aspect of our lives, never leaving our side for a second. If we ever feel alone, as if God is nowhere to be found, it is not because the Father has moved away from us, but we have in our minds moved away from Him. The believer needs to protect against these deceptive feelings by looking to God's Word and remembering the promises that Jesus Christ has made.

And surely I am with you always, to the very end of the age. (Matthew 28:20b NIV)

The Believer's Eternal Inheritance

In Christ, the inheritance waiting for us as the adopted children of God has been made possible and is preserved by the power of God in the heavenly realms (1 Peter 1:4-5). Although we will not fully understand the depths of this inheritance until we get to heaven, Peter gives us insight into its nature.

> *Blessed be the God and Father of our Lord Jesus Christ,*
> *who according to His great mercy has caused us to be born*
> *again to a living hope through the resurrection of Jesus*
> *Christ from the dead, to obtain an inheritance which is*
> *imperishable and undefiled and will not fade away,*
> *reserved in heaven for you, who are protected by the power*
> *of God through faith for a salvation ready to be revealed*
> *in the last time.* (1 Peter 1:3-5)

This inheritance is incorruptible and undefiled. It is not contaminated by sin or evil. Its essence is a reflection of everything God is in His holiness and righteousness. Perhaps the inheritance is the believer's confirmed holiness in the Lord forever. It will never fade or wear out; it is an eternal inheritance. Peter goes on to say that it is reserved in heaven for us, protected by the power of God. Heaven is the safe deposit box for our inheritance. The believer whose hope is in Jesus Christ lives his life knowing that the true treasures are awaiting him in heaven for all eternity.

THE ROLE OF THE HOLY SPIRIT

The role of the Holy Spirit is revealed to us in Ephesians 1:13-14:

> *In Him, you also, after listening to the message of truth,*
> *the gospel of your salvation—having also believed, you*
> *were sealed in Him with the Holy Spirit of promise, who is*
> *given as a pledge of our inheritance, with a view to the*
> *redemption of God's own possession, to the praise of His*
> *glory.*

Sealed with the Holy Spirit

The believer, in his heavenly calling, is sealed with the Holy Spirit of promise. The word *sealed* in Scripture carries the meaning of a finished transaction and depicts ownership (cf. Jeremiah 32:10-15) and security (Daniel 6:17). All three meanings in Scripture are true of the believer. The calling of the believer is a finished transaction. As far as God is concerned, the believer's past, present, and future history have already been mapped out. The believer's heavenly calling not only includes our salvation in Christ, but also takes us to the finish line where we, as God's children, will be glorified with Him for all eternity. This is strongly supported in Romans 8:29-30, where the past tense is used of glorification in describing the believer's call:

> *For those whom He foreknew, He also predestined to become conformed to the image of His Son, so that He would be the firstborn among many brethren; and these whom He predestined, He also called; and these whom He called, He also justified; and these whom He justified,* **He also glorified.** (emphasis added)

The sealing by the Holy Spirit also means that we are the property of God (ownership) and secured for all eternity. We are God's precious possession, set apart to enjoy the eternal fellowship of the Father with all the benefits and blessings He has bestowed on us.

This finished transaction and ownership is further developed in Ephesians 1:14. The Holy Spirit is the guarantee or *pledge* of our future inheritance. A pledge in its Greek usage carries the meaning of a part given in advance of what will be bestowed afterwards (money deposited by a purchaser in pledge of full payment). The bestowal of the Holy Spirit is God's pledge (deposit) or guarantee to the believer of the security and completeness of his salvation. This means the duration of this pledge is until the redemption of God's purchased possession, when we will be glorified in our new bodies for all eternity (see chapter 4).

The heavenly calling of the believer was not a sudden impulse by God reacting to something in the moment. The Father, Son, and Holy Spirit carefully planned it in eternity, reflecting the enormous love and grace that God has for us.

SUMMARY

Before leaving this chapter, it is beneficial to summarize the special interest and roles the Father, Son, and Holy Spirit have played in our heavenly calling. The Father has blessed us with every spiritual blessing in the heavenly places. He has chosen us before the creation of the earth with a purpose to be holy and blameless for all eternity. He has predestined us as part of His purpose to reveal the riches of His goodness. As adopted children of the Father we are given full rights to partake of His heavenly family with all the privileges and inheritance that are entitled to the children of God. The Son, through His sacrifice, has redeemed us from Satan's dominion and has forgiven our sins, lifting the barrier that had kept us separated from the Father. In the Son, we are given the mind of Christ (1 Corinthians 2:16), enlightened with all spiritual wisdom and knowledge, enabling us to comprehend the depths of God's holiness and righteousness. And finally, the Holy Spirit has sealed us, assuring us of our present and future blessings for all eternity. Praise the Lord!

Chapter Three

THE BELIEVER'S NEW STANDING UNDER GRACE

Therefore if anyone is in Christ, he is a new creature; the old things passed away; behold, new things have come. (2 Corinthians 5:17)

The believer who has experienced salvation has gone through an overhaul. This chapter calls attention to the changes that have taken place in our lives now that we have experienced the gift of salvation.

THE BELIEVER'S STANDING BEFORE SALVATION

In order to appreciate our new standing in Christ it would be wise to first reflect on what God has delivered us from. The believer before conversion was considered the enemy of God (Romans 5:10), who was at war with Him because of his sinful and fallen nature. The wrath of sin was a reality that hung over him for his rebellion against God. In this unrighteous state, we who are now believers, were once the pawns of Satan who carried out his diabolical plans in this world system that opposes everything God stands for. It wasn't our intention to promote his dominion, but because of our blindness and inability to understand spiritual matters and truth in our fallen nature, we were the instruments who carried out his lies that permeate and diminish the value of human society.

Rescued from the Dominion of Darkness

The Scriptures speak of four things believers have been delivered from in accepting Jesus Christ. In Colossians 1:13 we learn first that the believer has been rescued from the domain of darkness.

> *For He rescued us from the domain of darkness, and*
> *transferred us to the kingdom of His beloved Son, in*
> *whom we have redemption, the forgiveness of sins.*

This kingdom of darkness that is headed up by Satan has as its subjects those who have failed to put faith in Jesus Christ (the non-believing world). When the Son came into our hearts, the darkness that blinded us to truth was replaced by the light of Christ that illuminates holiness and righteousness; in effect, helping us flee from the deeds of darkness. The Apostle Paul admonished the believers in Ephesians to separate themselves from the darkness and walk according to the righteousness that is in the light.

> *Therefore do not be partakers with them; for you were for-*
> *merly darkness, but now you are Light in the Lord; walk*
> *as children of Light (for the fruit of the Light consists in all*
> *goodness and righteousness and truth), trying to learn*
> *what is pleasing to the Lord. Do not participate in the*
> *unfruitful deeds of darkness, but instead even expose*
> *them; for it is disgraceful even to speak of the things which*

are done by them in secret. But all things become visible
when they are exposed by the light, for everything that
becomes visible is light. For this reason it says,
"Awake, sleeper,
And arise from the dead,
And Christ will shine on you." (Ephesians 5:7-14)

Escaped the Corruption of the World

The second thing the Scriptures tell us of our deliverance is
that we have escaped the corruption of this world.

...seeing that His divine power has granted to us every-
thing pertaining to life and godliness, through the true
knowledge of Him who called us by His own glory and
excellence. For by these He has granted to us His precious
and magnificent promises, so that by them you may
become partakers of the divine nature, having escaped the
corruption that is in the world by lust. (2 Peter 1:3-4)

We have been freed from the bondage of Satan's dominion on
earth and no longer have to submit to his lies and diabolical ways.
We can now partake of our new divine nature that is in Christ,
escaping the corruption of our flesh that dominated our behavior under Satan's kingdom of darkness.

Freed from the Wrath of God

Third, we have been freed from the wrath of God for our sin,
which controlled us as children of darkness.

Much more then, having now been justified by His blood,
we shall be saved from the wrath of God through Him.
(Romans 5:9)

God's wrath towards our sin has been replaced by His abundant mercy and grace, which He freely pours out on us who trust in Jesus Christ for the forgiveness of our sins.

Freed from the Bondage of the Law

Fourth, we have been freed from the Law and united with Christ in our new standing with Him. The Law brought condemnation to all men (Romans 4:15), and was never intended to be a means of salvation for those who followed it. It was good and holy (Romans 7:12) and served as the standard of righteousness for the Old Testament saints, but it was limited in that it could not save or even sanctify a person in the practice of righteousness. The Law is perfect but this limitation was because of what the Law had to work with, which was sinful humanity, but its purpose was accomplished by revealing to the believer that he was a sinner and needed a savior. By putting faith in Jesus Christ, we are no longer under the authority of the Law that only brought death and not life. In Christ, we have died to the Law in order that we can walk in the newness of life that brings eternal life to those who believe.

> *Therefore, my brethren, you also were made to die to the Law through the body of Christ, so that you might be joined to another, to Him who was raised from the dead, in order that we might bear fruit for God. For while we were in the flesh, the sinful passions, which were aroused by the Law, were at work in the members of our body to bear fruit for death. But now we have been released from the Law, having died to that by which we were bound, so that we serve in newness of the Spirit and not in oldness of the letter.* (Romans 7:4-6)

THE NEW STANDING WITH THE FATHER

God has delivered us from this ungodly state of unrighteousness and has placed us into this new state of holiness, to be
blessed with Him, forever. Let us now consider our new standing as believers under grace. In relation to the Father, we have
moved out of the authority of Satan's dominion and control,
and have been *reconciled to the Father* through Jesus Christ
(Romans 5:10).

> *For if while we were enemies we were reconciled to God*
> *through the death of His Son, much more, having been*
> *reconciled, we shall be saved by His life. And not only this,*
> *but we also exult in God through our Lord Jesus Christ,*
> *through whom we have now received the reconciliation.*
> (Romans 5:10-11)

We have been transferred into God's kingdom under the
rulership of the Son (Colossians 1:13) to share in all His grace
and glory, not only presently but also throughout eternity.

> *For He rescued us from the domain of darkness, and*
> *transferred us to the kingdom of His beloved Son, in*
> *whom we have redemption, the forgiveness of sins.*
> (Colossians 1:13-14)

> *So that you would walk in a manner worthy of the*
> *God who calls you into His own kingdom and glory.*
> (1 Thessalonians 2:12)

As subjects of God's kingdom, we are the *personal posses-*
sion of the Father (1 Peter 2:9) and have been given a spiritual

priesthood in order to proclaim the greatness of God, upholding the truth of Christ against the enemies of the cross.

> But you are A CHOSEN RACE, A royal PRIESTHOOD, A HOLY
> NATION, A PEOPLE FOR God's OWN POSSESSION, so that you
> may proclaim the excellencies of Him who has called you
> out of darkness into His marvelous light; for you once were
> NOT A PEOPLE, but now you are THE PEOPLE OF GOD; you
> had NOT RECEIVED MERCY, but now you have RECEIVED
> MERCY. (1 Peter 2:9-10)

THE NEW STANDING WITH THE SON

In relationship to the Son in our new standing, we are *united with Jesus Christ* in his death, burial, and resurrection.

> Or do you not know that all of us who have been baptized
> into Christ Jesus have been baptized into His death?
> Therefore we have been buried with Him through baptism into death, so that as Christ was raised from the
> dead through the glory of the Father, so we too might
> walk in newness of life. For if we have become united with
> Him in the likeness of His death, certainly we shall also
> be in the likeness of His resurrection, knowing this, that
> our old self was crucified with Him, in order that our
> body of sin might be done away with, so that we would
> no longer be slaves to sin; for he who has died is freed
> from sin. (Romans 6:3-7)

Having been baptized into Christ's death, the believer is no longer under the slavery of sin but has been freed from its control in his new union with Christ. As Jesus Christ was crucified, buried, and resurrected, our flesh was crucified and buried in Him in order that we may live in the newness of our new life that has been raised up with Christ. We have become partakers in the life of Christ, no longer being subject to our sinful nature that has been rendered inoperative (Romans 6:6-7). We are made alive in Christ in order to live in the fullness of God's holiness and right-eousness. The Apostle Paul admonishes the believers to live according to this new life they have in Christ.

Therefore if you have been raised up with Christ, keep seeking the things above, where Christ is, seated at the right hand of God. Set your mind on the things above, not on the things that are on earth. For you have died and your life is hidden with Christ in God. When Christ, who is our life, is revealed, then you also will be revealed with Him in glory. (Colossians 3:1-4)

This new union of the believer with Christ is complete, not lacking anything of spiritual significance (Colossians 2:10). Therefore, there is nothing in this evil world which could over-come us, cause us to stumble or fall short of the task that God has given to us on this earth. We can now say no to ungodliness and worldly desires in the grace that God has provided.

For the grace of God has appeared, bringing salvation to all men, instructing us to deny ungodliness and worldly desires and to live sensibly, righteously and godly in the present age, looking for the blessed hope and the appearing of the glory of our great God and Savior, Christ Jesus, who gave Himself for us to redeem us from every lawless deed, and to purify for Himself a people for His own possession, zealous for good deeds. (Titus 2:11-14)

THE NEW STANDING WITH THE HOLY SPIRIT

In relation to the Holy Spirit, five things in the spiritual realm have become true of us at conversion. All five reveal the impact the promised Holy Spirit (John 14:16-17) has upon our Christian lives when we are born again.

Baptized by the Holy Spirit

First, the Holy Spirit has baptized all believers into the body of Christ, the church.

> *For even as the body is one and yet has many members, and all the members of the body, though they are many, are one body, so also is Christ. For by one Spirit **we were all baptized into one body,** whether Jews or Greeks, whether slaves or free, and we were all made to drink of one Spirit.* (1 Corinthians 12:12-13, emphasis added)

This baptism of the Holy Spirit is the means by which we are taken from a state of unrighteousness in the kingdom of darkness and brought into the body of Christ, the church, the kingdom of light. This also includes the fact that the believer is united with Christ in His burial and resurrection to partake in the life of Christ as a child of God.

> *Therefore we have been buried with Him through baptism into death, so that as Christ was raised from the dead through the glory of the Father, so we too might walk in newness of life. For if we have become united with Him in the likeness of His death, certainly we shall also be in the likeness of His resurrection, knowing this, that our old self was crucified with Him, in order that our*

body of sin might be done away with, so that we would
no longer be slaves to sin; for he who has died is freed
from sin. (Romans 6:4-7)

This is further reiterated in Colossians in which Paul relates Spirit baptism with the spiritual circumcision of Christ.

...and in Him you were also circumcised with a circumci-
sion made without hands, in the removal of the body of
the flesh by the circumcision of Christ; having been buried
with Him in baptism, in which you were also raised up
with Him through faith in the working of God, who raised
Him from the dead. When you were dead in your trans-
gressions and the uncircumcision of your flesh, He made
you alive together with Him, having forgiven us all our
transgressions, having canceled out the certificate of debt
consisting of decrees against us, which was hostile to us;
and He has taken it out of the way, having nailed it to the
cross. (Colossians 2:11-14)

Paul in this text is contrasting physical circumcision with the circumcision of the Spirit. Physical circumcision that was demanded under the Mosaic Law could not free the believer from the sin that dominates his life. In this spiritual circumcision, *"not done by human hands,"* we are made alive in Christ, freeing us from the old nature that was dead in transgressions. Our inability to overcome sin is replaced by the power of the Holy Spirit that enables us to walk in the holiness of God (Titus 2:12).

In Galatians, Paul emphasizes the fact that Spirit baptism is what identifies us as sons of God and one with Christ in His body.

For you are all sons of God through faith in Christ Jesus.
For all of you who were baptized into Christ have clothed
yourselves with Christ. There is neither Jew nor Greek, there
is neither slave nor free man, there is neither male nor
female; for you are all one in Christ Jesus. (Galatians 3:26-28)

Indwelt by the Holy Spirit

Second, is the permanent indwelling of the Holy Spirit, who
has taken up residency in our hearts (2 Timothy 1:14; Romans
8:9). He will never leave us or forsake us; He is always present in
our lives and will be with us forever. This is the promise that Jesus
made to the disciples before He departed and went to the Father.

I will ask the Father, and He will give you another Helper,
that He may be with you forever; that is the Spirit of
truth, whom the world cannot receive, because it does not
see Him or know Him, but you know Him because He
abides with you and will be in you. (John 14:16-17)

The Apostle Paul tells us that the indwelling of God's Holy
Spirit is an expression of His love for us.

...and hope does not disappoint, because the love of God
has been poured out within our hearts through the Holy
Spirit who was given to us. (Romans 5:5)

This indwelling is also the means by which we safeguard and
uphold the treasures of Scripture against the lies of the enemy.
Paul admonishes Timothy in this manner:

Retain the standard of sound words which you have heard
from me, in the faith and love which are in Christ Jesus.

Guard, through the Holy Spirit who dwells in us, *the*
treasure which has been entrusted to you. (2 Timothy 1:13-14,
emphasis added)

Regenerated by the Holy Spirit

Third, all believers have been regenerated by the Holy Spirit
according to Titus 3:5-6:

He saved us, not on the basis of deeds which we have done
in righteousness, but according to His mercy, by the wash-
ing of regeneration and renewing by the Holy Spirit,
whom He poured out upon us richly through Jesus Christ
our Savior.

I have often heard the expression, "You're one of those born
again Christians," yet each time I hear that, I say to myself, is there
any other kind? Born again was the expression used by Jesus in
His conversation with Nicodemus.

Jesus answered and said to him, "Truly, truly, I say to you,
unless one is born again he cannot see the kingdom of
God." (John 3:3)

It pointed out to Nicodemus that his knowledge of Jesus'
miracles (John 3:1-2) was not enough to make him a citizen of
God's Kingdom. Nicodemus must be made alive spiritually (born
again) in order to walk according to what he knew to be true in
the Scriptures. Nicodemus was on the right path, but unless he
received the ministry of the Holy Spirit *through repentance,*
which regenerates a person, he would remain in bondage to his
sinful nature. Those who are controlled by the sinful nature cannot please God (Romans 8:8). Many today, like Nicodemus,

believe their knowledge of Jesus Christ is a means of salvation *without repenting and putting faith in His atoning sacrifice.* They have a religious affiliation but have never been born again by turning from their sin and turning to God.

Regeneration emphasizes the born-again experience that is necessary for salvation. The meaning of *regeneration* is the impartation of spiritual life. The word itself stresses three changes that are true of us in salvation:

(1) The new birth of the believer:

> *Praise be to the God and Father of our Lord Jesus Christ! In his great mercy he has given us new birth into a living hope through the resurrection of Jesus Christ from the dead.* (1 Peter 1:3 NIV)

(2) The renewing by the Holy Spirit:

> *...he saved us, not because of righteous things we had done, but because of his mercy. He saved us through the washing of rebirth and renewal by the Holy Spirit.* (Titus 3:5 NIV)

(3) The new creation of the believer in Christ:

> *Therefore, if anyone is in Christ, he is a new creation; the old has gone, the new has come!* (2 Corinthians 5:17 NIV)

Regeneration gives us the ability to walk in the ways of God. We not only understand what the Bible is saying but we can live according to the spiritual life the Scriptures are demanding in God's children.

Sealed by the Holy Spirit

Fourth, the Holy Spirit has sealed all believers.

In Him, you also, after listening to the message of truth,
the gospel of your salvation—having also believed, you
were sealed in Him with the Holy Spirit of promise, who is
given as a pledge of our inheritance, with a view to the
redemption of God's own possession, to the praise of His
glory. (Ephesians 1:13-14)

The meaning and implication of the word *seal* were
addressed in chapter 2 under our heavenly calling in Christ. It
emphasized a finished transaction and ownership, which is true
of our heavenly calling. This sealing with the Spirit is the basis for
our security in salvation. The Holy Spirit is the guarantee or
pledge of our future inheritance in which we will be glorified and
secured forever. The believer can rejoice in the eternal redemption provided by God through the Holy Spirit. Our salvation is a
complete and finished transaction by God.

Anointed by the Holy Spirit

Fifth, all believers have been anointed by the Holy Spirit.

Now He who establishes us with you in Christ and
anointed us is God, who also sealed us and gave us the
Spirit in our hearts as a pledge. (2 Corinthians 1:21-22)

The Holy Spirit who indwells believers at salvation also
anointed us at that particular time. Although the word *anointing*
is used in many ways in the Old Testament, its usage in relation
to the New Testament believer carries this meaning, the ability to
understand and act upon spiritual truth. The anointing is the

basis for comprehending the truths of God's Word (cf. John 2:20-27; 1 Corinthians 2:14-16).

> *But you have an anointing from the Holy One, and all of you know the truth.* (1 John 2:20 NIV)

> *As for you, the anointing you received from him remains in you, and you do not need anyone to teach you. But as his anointing teaches you about all things and as that anointing is real, not counterfeit—just as it has taught you, remain in him.* (1 John 2:27 NIV)

This anointing is also the means by which we develop deep convictions for what we know to be true. Before receiving the Holy Spirit in salvation, we could only comprehend the Scriptures in an intellectual capacity, without fully understanding the spiritual depths revealed in them. But now through the anointing of the Holy Spirit, we can understand the depths of His Word from a spiritual perspective, for we have *"the mind of Christ"* (1 Corinthians 2:16). As the believer responds in obedience through this anointing, he develops firm convictions that are necessary to stand and act upon the truths of Scripture (cf. 1 Thessalonians 1:5). He is fully persuaded in his heart to walk according to the Word of God.

While many pray for an anointing upon someone who is about to teach or instruct, the reality is, according to New Testament Scripture, all believers in Christ have been anointed once and for all (1 John 2:20). Even to suggest that one believer is anointed and another believer needs the anointing is biblically incorrect. This is why you never see a request for the anointing on someone in New Testament writings. When we received the gift of the Holy Spirit at salvation, the anointing was included in the package, which is the theological truth of the matter.

All five of these, the baptism, the indwelling, the regeneration, the sealing, and the anointing of the Holy Spirit have become a reality in the believer's conversion and new standing under grace. God provides these ministries of the Holy Spirit to empower us for service in witnessing to the truth of the gospel message.

> *But you will receive power when the Holy Spirit comes on you; and you will be my witnesses in Jerusalem, and in all Judea and Samaria, and to the ends of the earth.* (Acts 1:8 NIV)

SUMMARY

In review, the believer has been delivered from Satan's domain of darkness that had blinded us from the truth of God, has escaped the corruption of the world that fed our sinful nature, has been freed from the wrath of sin that hung over us while we were still sinners, and has been freed from the law that brought condemnation. In delivering us from this state of unrighteousness, God has brought us into a new standing with Him that will continue for all eternity. In relation to the Father, the believer has been reconciled by being made acceptable through Christ. We are transferred into God's kingdom and glory and brought under the rule of the Son, Jesus Christ. We have become the personal possession of God as His adopted children and citizens of heaven for all eternity.

In relation to the Son, we have been united with Christ in His death, burial, and resurrection. Our sinful nature that ruled our inner being was crucified and buried with Christ when we put faith in Him. We are raised up in the newness of life, becoming partakers in the life of Jesus Christ, and equipped to live in the fullness of holiness and righteousness that was given to us at conversion. This transformation from the old nature to the new is complete in Christ (positional truth), lacking nothing, in order that we may live as children of light testifying to the truth of God in every part of our being.

The Holy Spirit has baptized us into the body of Christ that we may partake of the life of Christ. We are permanently indwelt by the Holy Spirit and regenerated, giving us the spiritual capacity to follow in the will of God. We are secured in our salvation by the sealing ministry of the Holy Spirit and anointed for service, through which we learn the depths of God's truth and develop firm convictions in upholding God's Word. Take joy my brothers and sisters in what God has bestowed upon us. Amen!

Chapter Four

THE MIRACLE OF SALVATION; FROM JUSTIFICATION TO GLORIFICATION

For those whom He foreknew, He also predestined to become conformed to the image of His son, so that He would be the firstborn among many brethren; and these whom He predestined, He also called; and these whom He called, He also justified; and these whom He justified, He also glorified. (Romans 8:29-30)

In the above passage we learn that the Father in our salvation has predestined us to be conformed to the image of His Son, Jesus Christ. Our salvation includes being justified at conversion and glorified for all eternity. The believer's salvation is a completed work by the Father in heaven. Salvation is truly a miracle when one considers the aspects of salvation that perfect the believer for all eternity.

This chapter demonstrates the riches of God's grace and love to the believer by tracing the three aspects of salvation: *justification, sanctification, and glorification.* All three reveal the grace of God in delivering the believer from the penalty and power of sin, forever.

JUSTIFICATION

In justification, the believer is declared righteous before God, innocent of any guilt incurred by sin. It is a gift of God by grace in which we stand vindicated before the Father in relation to sin.

> *But now apart from the Law the righteousness of God has been manifested, being witnessed by the Law and the Prophets, even the righteousness of God through faith in Jesus Christ for all those who believe; for there is no distinction; for all have sinned and fall short of the glory of God,* **being justified as a gift by His grace** *through the redemption which is in Christ Jesus.* (Romans 3:21-24, emphasis added)

We are delivered from the penalty of sin by one act of faith in God. The believer can do nothing through his own works to be justified before God. He needs only to deposit his full trust in Jesus Christ by faith. Salvation is believing, not achieving, therefore works play no role in the justifying process. The reason for this is the basis for justification; God has provided all the work necessary for salvation (cf. John 6:29) through the death and resurrection of Jesus Christ.

This first aspect of salvation, justification, is not a process that continues to repeat itself, but is a one-time act that occurs at a definite time in the believer's life. This is supported by the Greek tense in Scripture, which always portrays justification as a past reality in the believer's life (cf. Romans 5:1). Once and for all, the believer is justified before God, delivered from the penalty of sin; therefore, justification emphasizes the past aspect of our salvation.

SANCTIFICATION

In sanctification, the believer is delivered from the power of sin in his daily life. This aspect emphasizes the *present reality* of salvation in which the believer is being sanctified and renewed on a daily basis.

There are two facets to this sanctifying aspect, *positional* sanctification and *progressive* sanctification. Positional sanctification stresses the fact that the believer has been brought into a permanent position to be sanctified by God. This means the believer is completely set apart from this evil world and designated for God's personal use in promoting righteousness on the earth. We are the instruments or ambassadors of God, who have been delivered from ungodliness in order to represent God and penetrate the darkness of this world. The Holy Spirit is the agent or means through whom we enter into positional sanctification (cf. Romans 15:16; 2 Thessalonians 2:13; 1 Peter 1:2).

Progressive sanctification stresses the everyday work of the Holy Spirit in the believer's life. This aspect is a process that continues throughout the life of the believer until he is joined with Christ at death or through the Rapture of the church (cf. 1 Thessalonians 4:13-17). The Father accomplishes this sanctifying process through the work of the Holy Spirit (cf. Romans 8:12-13; Ephesians 3:16). The obligation of the believer in this process is to be obedient to the Word of God and sensitive to the guidance of the Holy Spirit in his life (see chapter 7). When the Holy Spirit is able to lead in this manner, the believer is sanctified daily, growing in his Christian walk and reaching maturity in the faith. This progressive sanctifying aspect of salvation is emphasized in Philippians 2:12-13:

So then, my beloved, just as you have always obeyed, not as in my presence only, but now much more in my absence, work out your salvation with fear and trembling; for it is God who is at work in you, both to will and to work for His good pleasure.

In this text the believer is called to *work out*, not work for his salvation; that is, to walk in the salvation which has already been provided at conversion by the believer's faith in Christ. There are no works necessary to earn our salvation. Salvation is the gift of God to those who put faith in Christ (cf. Romans 4:2-5). Works enter into the picture after we have received salvation. We are obligated to produce the works and deeds of righteousness as members of the body of Christ, the church. This is possible because God has equipped us with all the resources necessary to do His will at salvation (see chapter 3). It is now a matter of going on to maturity by being sanctified by the Holy Spirit on a daily basis in our Christian faith.

This sanctifying aspect needs to be distinguished from the justifying aspect of salvation. If not, a believer will be under the impression that his holiness, *the believer's perfect standing before God,* is maintained or affected by the way he conducts himself in everyday life. Holiness is determined by our faith in Christ, who is our righteousness.

But by His doing you are in Christ Jesus, who became to us wisdom from God, and righteousness and sanctification, and redemption. (1 Corinthians 1:30)

It is Christ in us who has made us holy and blameless (perfect) before the Father in salvation. God sees repentant sinners in the holiness and righteousness of Christ. When we were justified in salvation, our position in holiness had been determined; therefore, our conduct does not determine our holiness.

It is the sanctifying work of the Holy Spirit that is helping the believer express the holiness of God, which has become our possession through Jesus Christ in salvation. Therefore, progressive sanctification requires the believer to uphold his obligation to his calling in Christ. He or she is to walk in obedience and be sensitive to the convicting power of the Holy Spirit (See page 72) that makes us aware of the sin in our lives. The believer who is sanctified daily will reach maturity. Whereas, all believers are perfect in their new standing before God, maturity in the faith is the difference between believers in their Christian walk. Some will mature to greater degrees than others because of their obedience to the leading of the Holy Spirit.

Our faithfulness to our calling in the body of Christ will determine the rewards we will receive at the judgment seat of Christ.

For we must all appear before the judgment seat of Christ,
so that each one may be recompensed for his deeds in the
body, according to what he has done, whether good or bad.
(2 Corinthians 5:10)

This judgment is not for the sins we have committed—they were dealt with at the cross—but for the works or deeds we have produced as children of God under the sanctifying process of the Holy Spirit. Jesus Christ will examine our faithfulness to our calling and reward us according to our deeds done in the body of Christ. This is the point the Apostle Paul is making in 1 Corinthians 3:10-15:

According to the grace of God which was given to me, like
a wise master builder I laid a foundation, and another is

building on it. But each man must be careful how he builds on it. For no man can lay a foundation other than the one which is laid, which is Jesus Christ. Now if any man builds on the foundation with gold, silver, precious stones, wood, hay, straw, each man's work will become evident; for the day will show it because it is to be revealed with fire, and the fire itself will test the quality of each man's work. If any man's work which he has built on it remains, he will receive a reward. If any man's work is burned up, he will suffer loss; but he himself will be saved, yet so as through fire.

To understand passages like this and others (cf. 2 Corinthians 5:10; Philippians 2:12-13), we must emphasize the second aspect of our salvation, sanctification (progressive). If not, we will do an injustice to our new standing in Christ (positional truth) by believing that our works for God put us in a better position or standing with Him. Our standing with God has been determined by the gift of salvation through faith, which includes the righteousness of Christ in us and does not change. Failure to go on to maturity in our new standing will result in a loss of rewards but not affect the position of the believer. In saying that, what believer would want to go before the Father knowing that he failed to give God his best while here on earth.

GLORIFICATION

Glorification is the future aspect of salvation in which we are delivered from the presence of sin for all eternity. This is the finished product of our salvation. The believer will receive a new, glorified body that is conducive to his future eternal abode with Christ.

For our citizenship is in heaven, from which also we
eagerly wait for a Savior, the Lord Jesus Christ; who will
transform the body of our humble state into conformity
with the body of His glory, by the exertion of the power
that He has even to subject all things to Himself
(Philippians 3:20-21)

The Rapture of the church, when Christ comes back for the believers, will inaugurate this future aspect of salvation. This will fulfill the promise of Christ that was made during His earthly ministry to the disciples.

Do not let your heart be troubled; believe in God, believe
also in Me. "In My Father's house are many dwelling
places; if it were not so, I would have told you; for I go to
prepare a place for you. "If I go and prepare a place for
you, I will come again and receive you to Myself, that
where I am, there you may be also (John 14:1-3).

This promise is reiterated in the writings of the Apostle Paul to the church at Thessalonica with the emphasis put on the way it will happen.

But we do not want you to be uninformed, brethren,
about those who are asleep, so that you will not grieve as
do the rest who have no hope. For if we believe that Jesus
died and rose again, even so God will bring with Him
those who have fallen asleep in Jesus. For this we say to
you by the word of the Lord, that we who are alive and
remain until the coming of the Lord, will not precede
those who have fallen asleep. For the Lord Himself will
descend from heaven with a shout, with the voice of the

archangel and with the trumpet of God, and the dead in Christ will rise first. Then we who are alive and remain will be caught up together with them in the clouds to meet the Lord in the air, and so we shall always be with the Lord. Therefore comfort one another with these words. (1 Thessalonians 4:13-18)

When Christ comes back for His church, believers will be given their glorified bodies. Those who have died preceding this event will be united with their glorified bodies at the Rapture of the church. The generation that experiences the coming of Christ for his church will go through a transformation by which their human bodies will be caught up in the air, changed in an instant and take on their glorified bodies.

Behold, I tell you a mystery; we will not all sleep, but we will all be changed, in a moment, in the twinkling of an eye, at the last trumpet; for the trumpet will sound, and the dead will be raised imperishable, and we will be changed. (1 Corinthians 15:51-52)

THE ASSURANCE OF GLORIFICATION

The assurance of our glorification is revealed to us in Romans 8:28-39. This assurance is reinforced in four different ways. The first is the nature of God's call on our lives (8:28-30).

And we know that God causes all things to work together for good to those who love God, to those who are called according to His purpose. For those whom He foreknew, He also predestined to become conformed to the image of His Son, so that He would be the firstborn among many

brethren; and these whom He predestined, He also called;
and these whom He called, He also justified; and these
whom He justified, He also glorified.

God's calling upon our lives, which was ordained before we ever took our first breath, is a finished work that includes our future glorification. This is strongly implied in verse 30 where the past tense, "he also glorified" is used to describe this future aspect of our salvation. As far as God is concerned, we have been glorified for all eternity.

The second reason for the assurance of our glorification is the nature of salvation, verses 31 and 32:

What then shall we say to these things? If God is for us,
who is against us? He who did not spare His own Son, but
delivered Him over for us all, how will He not also with
Him freely give us all things?

It is Almighty God who orchestrated our salvation through the death of His only Son at the cross, while we were enemies of His. If this is true, how much more will the Father in heaven provide for us as His children, in freely bestowing His unending love and grace. Putting this in prospective, if God loved us enough to save us as His enemies who were actively sinning against Him in our fallen nature, how much more will God's love provide for us, now that we are His children.

The third assurance of this future aspect is the nature of justification, verses 33 and 34:

Who will bring a charge against God's elect? God is the
one who justifies; who is the one who condemns? Christ

Jesus is He who died, yes, rather who was raised, who is at the right hand of God, who also intercedes for us.

Christ, who died for us in order to justify us before the Father, now lives to intercede for us as our High Priest in heaven at the right hand of God (see chapter 5). Who can now bring any charges against those who God has justified? Christ our *advocate* (cf. 1 John 2:1-2) continuously defends our justified standing before the Father against any accusations that are made, including those made by Satan (cf. Revelation 12:9-11).

The fourth assurance of our glorification is the nature of God's love.

Who will separate us from the love of Christ? Will tribulation, or distress, or persecution, or famine, or nakedness, or peril, or sword? Just as it is written,
"FOR YOUR SAKE WE ARE BEING PUT TO DEATH ALL DAY LONG; WE WERE CONSIDERED AS SHEEP TO BE SLAUGHTERED."
But in all these things we overwhelmingly conquer through Him who loved us. For I am convinced that neither death, nor life, nor angels, nor principalities, nor things present, nor things to come, nor powers, nor height, nor depth, nor any other created thing, will be able to separate us from the love of God, which is in Christ Jesus our Lord. (Romans 8:35-39)

There is nothing in all creation that can separate the believer from the love of God. We as God's children are the recipients of this never-ending love that protects us and will be with us for all eternity. God's infinite love is an ongoing reality that is included in the riches of the believer in the eternal calling of our salvation.

SUMMARY

In review, there are three aspects of salvation: justification, sanctification, and glorification. As far as God's calling on our lives, we have already been justified, sanctified, and glorified (positional truth) in our new standing with the Father. In justification, we are declared righteous (made perfect in Christ) and freed from the penalty of sin. We are set apart in sanctification as God's holy instruments in order to go on to spiritual maturity (progressive sanctification) and live in a manner that reflects our new standing in Christ. We have been glorified from God's perspective in salvation. When Christ comes back for His church, we will receive new glorified bodies and reign with Him, fellowshipping with the Father, the Son, and the Holy Spirit for all eternity.

Chapter Five

THE PRESENT MINISTRY OF JESUS CHRIST AND THE HOLY SPIRIT

I will ask the Father, and He will give you another Helper, that He may be with you forever; that is the Spirit of truth, whom the world cannot receive, because it does not see Him or know Him, but you know Him because He abides with you and will be in you.

"I will not leave you as orphans; I will come to you. "After a little while the world will no longer see Me, but you will see Me; because I live, you will live also. "In that day you will know that I am in My Father, and you in Me, and I in you. "He who has My commandments and keeps them is the one who loves Me; and he who loves Me will be loved by My Father, and I will love him and will disclose Myself to him." (John 14:16-21)

This promise by Jesus Christ reveals the fact that as His disciples, we will never be alone in the present reality of our salvation. The Holy Spirit abides in us along with the immediate presence of the Son, who loves us and intercedes for our continual well-being in our Christian walk. In this chapter, we will examine the present roles of Jesus Christ and the Holy Spirit in supplying us with all of the necessary assistance that goes along with our new standing in salvation.

THE PRESENT MINISTRY OF THE SON

The book of Hebrews has sometimes been called the fifth gospel because it portrays the present ministry of Jesus Christ in heaven, whereas the four gospels speak about His earthly ministry. Perhaps in other terms it could be called the sequel to the gospels because it takes us beyond them and reveals to us the things that are true in His present ministry. When Jesus Christ said at the cross in the Gospel of John, "*It is finished*," John 19:30, He meant that His purpose in taking on humanity was completed in relationship to sin. He had paid in full the price for the penalty of sin, enabling all of those who put faith in Him to be reconciled to the Father in salvation. When He departed He began His new ministry in heaven as our High Priest at the right hand of God. The book of Hebrews portrays this precious ministry of Christ in heaven on behalf of those who look to Him for grace and mercy in time of need. By examining the pertinent truths of this magnificent book, we see how the Son is fulfilling His promise in never forsaking us in this great salvation provided by God.

In order to appreciate the ministry of Christ and what He means to the church saint, the author of Hebrews, who is speaking to Jewish believers, shows the superiority of Christ in His ministry over the Old Covenant and its Levitical priesthood. The Jewish believers addressed in Hebrews were returning to the old practice of the Mosaic Law and, in so doing, failed to see the role of Jesus Christ in their new standing by faith. These Jewish believers needed to refocus and put their eyes on Jesus Christ, in order to realize the awesomeness of His role in helping them mature in the faith and endure the persecution, hardships, and tribulations of this life. If they failed to make this adjustment they would not live in the fullness of their Christian lives, going back to a life in Judaism that would keep them stagnant and unable to grow (cf. Hebrews 5:11-12). They would fail to trust in the finished work of the Son at the cross through obedience, which is necessary in order to perfect the righteousness of Christ that is in all believers.

The author of Hebrews begins his epistle by showing the *superiority of the Son* over the prophets, the angels, and Moses, who are considered the pillars of Judaism (Hebrews 1:1-3:6). As great as these three pillars were to the divine religion of the Jews before Christ, they fade in comparison to the glory of the Son in His person and ministry on behalf of the church saint. The author's objective is to draw the Jewish believers' attention to Christ, who far exceeds in glory any items of Judaism that had been considered great. A common expression that runs throughout the book of Hebrews is, *"consider Jesus"* (Hebrews 3:1, 12:3).

Pursuing his theme, the author shows the superiority of Christ over the old practices of the Law. By contrasting the Levitical priesthood under the Law with the perfect and eternal ministry of Jesus Christ, the superiority of the Son is clearly seen. Jesus Christ is superior in His calling (Hebrews 5:1-10), His priesthood (Hebrews 7:1-17), and His ministry (Hebrews 8:1-10:39). He ministers on behalf of the believer, in a better position (Hebrews 8:1), in a heavenly tabernacle (Hebrews 8:2-5), under a better covenant (Hebrews 8:6-9:10), and with a better sacrifice, which was His own life (Hebrews 9:11-10:18). There is no substitute for the Son when it comes to ministering on behalf of the believer.

Chapter 10 brings the author's powerful testimony of Jesus Christ to a conclusion. He begins by reminding the believers of the weakness and temporary nature of the Law.

*For the Law, since it has only a shadow of the good things
to come and not the very form of things, can never, by
the same sacrifices which they offer continually year by
year, make perfect those who draw near. Otherwise,
would they not have ceased to be offered, because the
worshipers, having once been cleansed, would no longer
have had consciousness of sins? But in those sacrifices
there is a reminder of sins year by year. For it is impossible for the blood of bulls and goats to take away sins.*
(Hebrews 10:1-4)

Under the former system, the worshippers could never enter
into the Holy of Holies or even the Tabernacle itself, showing
the approach to God in worship was still limited in many ways.
Their sins were never completely removed and they constantly
had to bring an offering to the priest in order to stay in fellowship with God, but now in Christ the believer has been made
perfect in his new standing with God. He can approach the
Father unhindered by sin in order to receive grace and mercy in
times of weakness.

*And every priest stands daily ministering and offering time
after time the same sacrifices, which can never take away
sins; but He, having offered one sacrifice for sins for all
time, SAT DOWN AT THE RIGHT HAND OF GOD, waiting from
that time onward UNTIL HIS ENEMIES BE MADE A FOOTSTOOL
FOR HIS FEET. For by one offering He has perfected for all
time those who are sanctified.* (Hebrews 10:11-14)

The author of Hebrews concludes this theme of the superiority of Jesus Christ with applications that bring the believer face to
face with this reality.

Therefore, brethren, since we have confidence to enter the holy place by the blood of Jesus, by a new and living way which He inaugurated for us through the veil, that is, His flesh, and since we have a great priest over the house of God, let us draw near with a sincere heart in full assurance of faith, having our hearts sprinkled clean from an evil conscience and our bodies washed with pure water. Let us hold fast the confession of our hope without wavering, for He who promised is faithful; and let us consider how to stimulate one another to love and good deeds, not forsaking our own assembling together, as is the habit of some, but encouraging one another; and all the more as you see the day drawing near. (Hebrews 10:19-25)

Today we need to fully comprehend the place of Jesus Christ in our salvation, who is our hope and strength in our faith. The believer has full access in Jesus Christ to the throne of grace, *the Heavenly Holy of Holies*, and can approach the Father with confidence, no longer needing animal sacrifices or any human mediator (the Levitical priest) to partake of this privileged position. Jesus is our High Priest in heaven interceding on our behalf and making it possible for us to live victorious Christian lives. He is the channel through which God pours out His grace and mercy upon us in order to have victory over sin and to persevere and endure through the trials and tribulations of everyday life. His sacrifice, which was once and for all, brought eternal forgiveness to our lives. We will never again be separated from the Father because of sin. As our High Priest, He identifies with our temptations and weaknesses in order that He can comfort us and strengthen us in our daily lives.

But Jesus the Son of God is our great High Priest who has gone to heaven itself to help us; therefore let us never stop trusting him. This High Priest of ours understands our weaknesses since he had the same temptations we do, though he never once gave way to them and sinned. So let us come boldly to the very throne of God and stay there to receive his mercy and to find grace to help us in our times of need. (Hebrews 4:14-16 TLB)

Because He lives, He always intercedes for us at the right hand of the Father, never forsaking us in our moment of need.

...but Jesus, on the other hand, because He continues forever, holds His priesthood permanently. Therefore He is able also to save forever those who draw near to God through Him, since He always lives to make intercession for them. (Hebrews 7:24-25)

He has broken down every barrier between God and the believer that prevented us from experiencing the abundant life the Father so willingly bestowed on us. Therefore, we as God's children have no external obstacles preventing us from entering into the fullness of God's love, grace, and mercy that is always available through our High Priest, Jesus Christ. The only stumbling block is our lack of faith to believe in the finished work of Christ and all of the blessings that have become our possession. Our Christian life began with faith and our Christian life obligates us to continue in faith until Christ comes back to take us home (cf. Romans 1:17). The Apostle Paul, understanding the believer's need for faith in the Christian walk, prayed for the saints in this manner.

For this reason I bow my knees before the Father, from whom every family in heaven and on earth derives its

name, that He would grant you, according to the riches of
His glory, to be strengthened with power through His
Spirit in the inner man, **so that Christ may dwell in your**
hearts through faith; *and that you, being rooted and*
grounded in love, may be able to comprehend with all the
saints what is the breadth and length and height and
depth, and to know the love of Christ which surpasses
knowledge, that you may be filled up to all the fullness of
God. (Ephesians 3:14-19, emphasis added)

By exercising faith, we are in effect recognizing the awesome role of Christ in our daily lives and receiving the utmost benefit of His ministry as our High Priest. Apart from abiding in Christ as our High Priest, the believer can do nothing to produce the fruits of righteousness. This was what Jesus Christ was alluding to in the Gospel of John.

Abide in Me, and I in you. As the branch cannot bear fruit
of itself unless it abides in the vine, so neither can you unless
you abide in Me. "I am the vine, you are the branches; he
who abides in Me and I in him, he bears much fruit, for
apart from Me you can do nothing. (John 15:4-5)

To abide in Christ is to obey and trust in Him with all of our heart, not wavering in the faith. He is the source of all our strength and growth. The believer who trusts God in this way has the firm conviction that God is able to do what He has said in His Word. This kind of faith enables us to enter into God's rest, free from the worries and anxieties of life that choke off our belief in God. Apart from Him there is no rest for the believer. This was the warning to the Jewish believers of Hebrews 3:7- 4:10, who were about to commit the same mistake of the wilderness generation of Exodus, who failed to enter into God's blessings and rest because of unbelief.

> *Beware then of your own hearts, dear brothers, lest you find that they, too, are evil and unbelieving and are leading you away from the living God. Speak to each other about these things every day while there is still time so that none of you will become hardened against God, being blinded by the glamor of sin. For if we are faithful to the end, trusting God just as we did when we first became Christians, we will share in all that belongs to Christ. But now is the time. Never forget the warning, "Today if you hear God's voice speaking to you, do not harden your hearts against him, as the people of Israel did when they rebelled against him in the desert."* (Hebrews 3:12-15 TLB)

The generation of Moses' day had experienced the wonders and reality of God at the Red Sea; nevertheless, they failed to trust in God in the aftermath of their awesome deliverance from Egypt. Instead of experiencing everything God had promised them through Moses, they ended up in the wilderness for forty years outside the blessings of God as they wandered around unable to enter into God's rest. In the same way, the believers in the church who fail to come to Christ and live by faith will fail to experience the full benefits of His role as our High Priest. The believer will wander or stumble through this life never entering into the abundant life that God has given him in Jesus Christ.

It is one thing to believe in the testimony of the Son for salvation, but it is another thing to trust in Him on a daily basis for our daily needs. When the latter is true, then the believer will enter into God's rest, experiencing the joy, peace, and righteousness that God provides in the Holy Spirit in this life (cf. Romans 14:17).

The degree to which a believer trusts Jesus Christ in his faith will distinguish a mature Christian from one who remains a babe in the faith. The believer is called to *consider Jesus*, our High Priest and mediator at the right hand of the Father in heaven.

THE PRESENT MINISTRY OF THE HOLY SPIRIT

The believer not only has God the Son working on his behalf, but also the Holy Spirit. In chapter 3, we learned of the past reality of the Holy Spirit in our salvation, in which all believers had been baptized, indwelt, regenerated, sealed, and anointed by the Holy Spirit at that moment. But just as the Son has a present role in our lives, so too the Holy Spirit continually ministers on our behalf in order for us to walk in the fullness of our calling.

Teaching and Illuminating Spiritual Truth

The first ministry the Holy Spirit provides in our present Christian walk is to teach us spiritual truths.

> For who among men knows the thoughts of a man except the spirit of the man which is in him? Even so the thoughts of God no one knows except the Spirit of God. Now we have received, not the spirit of the world, but the Spirit who is from God, so that we may know the things freely given to us by God, which things we also speak, not in words taught by human wisdom, but in those taught by the Spirit, combining spiritual thoughts with spiritual words. But a natural man does not accept the things of the Spirit of God, for they are foolishness to him; and he cannot understand them, because they are spiritually appraised. But he who is spiritual appraises all things, yet he himself is appraised by no one. For WHO HAS KNOWN

THE MIND OF THE LORD, THAT HE WILL INSTRUCT HIM? *But we have the mind of Christ.* (1 Corinthians 2:11-16)

The believer, who is indwelt by the Holy Spirit, discerns all things that come from the Father. He is able to understand the depths of God's Word with the wisdom that comes from the Spirit. This is possible because the Holy Spirit illuminates in our minds and hearts the meaning of the Scriptures as we read and apply them in our lives. The text above reveals how the unbeliever, *the man without the Spirit,* cannot discern the intended meaning or thrust of a text and its spiritual value. He can read Scripture, but the spiritual value it provides in understanding God's heart is foreign to his natural tendencies in his fallen nature.

We believers, who are born again and indwelt by the Holy Spirit, have taken on a new mindset through our conversion. Not only do we now want to please God, but our perspectives on issues pertaining to holiness and righteousness have changed as well. In this new state of mind and heart, we are made aware of all the treasures of life that are truly meaningful and precious to God. They include, a genuine love that is expressed in a deep concern for others, a standard of righteousness in Christ that exceeds any standard set up by man, and a value system that operates in humility and understands greatness from God's perspective.

The greatest among you will be your servant. (Matthew 23:11)

Love, righteousness, and humility are characteristics that escape man in his natural mind. Through the illuminating ministry of the Holy Spirit, the eyes and hearts of the born-again believer are opened to these meaningful riches of life.

Direction and Guidance

Second, the Holy Spirit provides direction in our lives. God leads His people on the right path by the guidance of the Holy Spirit.

For all who are being led by the Spirit of God, these are sons of God. (Romans 8:14)

God has provided this present ministry of the Spirit to help us make the right decisions as His children. When the Holy Spirit guides us, we grow spiritual antennas in order to know the direction that God is leading. Examples of this guiding ministry are given to us throughout the book of Acts (8:29; 10:19-20; 11:12; 13:2-4: 16:6-10). This ministry of the Holy Spirit is effected in the believer as one seeks the will of God in promoting His kingdom of righteousness upon this earth.

But seek first His kingdom and His righteousness, and all these things will be added to you. (Matthew 6:33)

If this is the desire of our heart, to seek God's kingdom and glorify the Father with our lives, how can God withhold His will from us who look to Him through the Holy Spirit for direction?

Sometimes the direction we are looking for is not as precise as we want it to be. There are decisions in life in which we need to make a choice between two or three alternatives. This is especially true when choosing a job or going into the ministry. When our priorities are right in seeking God's kingdom first, we can trust in the Lord to direct us in these uncertain moments. God has an uncanny way of directing our lives when we are not fully sure of the right course of action. As long as the believer maintains a proper heart, the will of the Father will be perfected through this guiding ministry of the Holy Spirit. The believer will find himself walking on the right path, discerning the will of God for his life.

Conviction upon the Believer's Heart

The third work of the Holy Spirit in the present is the convicting ministry of the Spirit to bring change upon our character and behavior. As the Holy Spirit leads us by conviction, He impresses upon our hearts what is proper and right in our conduct before God. This conviction is necessary to make godly changes as righteous ambassadors of God's kingdom on earth. This conviction not only makes us aware of our shortcomings, but sensitive to the things that are pure and righteous in God's sight. Those who are led by the Holy Spirit in this manner do not carry out the desires of the flesh but rather the desires of the Father, producing the fruit of the Spirit in all manner of life.

> But I say, walk by the Spirit, and you will not carry out the desire of the flesh. For the flesh sets its desire against the Spirit, and the Spirit against the flesh; for these are in opposition to one another, so that you may not do the things that you please. But if you are led by the Spirit, you are not under the Law. Now the deeds of the flesh are evident, which are: immorality, impurity, sensuality, idolatry, sorcery, enmities, strife, jealousy, outbursts of anger, disputes, dissensions, factions, envying, drunkenness, carousing, and things like these, of which I forewarn you, just as I have forewarned you, that those who practice such things will not inherit the kingdom of God. But the fruit of the Spirit is love, joy, peace, patience, kindness, goodness, faithfulness, gentleness, self-control; against such things

there is no law. Now those who belong to Christ Jesus have crucified the flesh with its passions and desires. If we live by the Spirit, let us also walk by the Spirit. Let us not become boastful, challenging one another, envying one another. (Galatians 5:16-26)

The key to the above passage is that we are no longer under the Law (verse 18). Those who try to walk according to the Law will arouse the sinful desires of the flesh; but we who have died to the Law (see chapter two) are no longer under its jurisdiction, but under the control and power of the Holy Spirit. This was the point the Apostle Paul made in Romans 7 and 8 where he found himself struggling with sin. He realized that he needed to live under grace by the Spirit of life and not under law.

Therefore there is now no condemnation for those who are in Christ Jesus. For the law of the Spirit of life in Christ Jesus has set you free from the law of sin and of death. For what the Law could not do, weak as it was through the flesh, God did: sending His own Son in the likeness of sinful flesh and as an offering for sin, He condemned sin in the flesh, so that the requirement of the Law might be fulfilled in us, who do not walk according to the flesh but according to the Spirit. For those who are according to the flesh set their minds on the things of the flesh, but those who are according to the Spirit, the things of the Spirit. (Romans 8:1-5)

If we choose to live a Spirit-led life, by way of conviction, the requirements of righteousness will be produced in us as the Holy Spirit helps us to identify with right and wrong. This is accomplished by simply acknowledging in humility the prompting of the Holy Spirit in bringing conviction upon our hearts when there is need for change in our lives. As we respond to the conviction of the Holy Spirit by calling upon the Lord for change, the unrighteousness that is in us will be uprooted. If we have sinned, conviction leads us to confess our sin to the Father. If we are struggling in weaknesses or addictions, conviction causes us to cry out for deliverance. If we are lukewarm, godly conviction stirs up our hearts to cry out for revival. God hears the cries of His people who are sincerely looking for change in their lives. The Father is faithful in answering the prayers of His children, especially those that are requesting to turn from ungodliness. Do not smolder the voice of God when He is speaking to you by the convicting power of the Holy Spirit. This ministry of the Holy Spirit is a powerful means of growing in the grace of God.

Assurance of God's Love

Fourth, the Holy Spirit provides assurance of God's love for His children. The Holy Spirit testifies with our hearts that we belong to God.

> *The Spirit Himself testifies with our spirit that we are children of God.* (Romans 8:16)

> *Because you are sons, God has sent forth the Spirit of His Son into our hearts, crying, "Abba! Father!"* (Galatians 4:6)

This ministry of assurance by the Holy Spirit is vital to us as Christians. The enemy, Satan, is working overtime misrepresenting the Father's never ending-love and concern for us. He is using the same tactics he used in the Garden of Eden when he deceived Eve into questioning God's Word.

Now the serpent was more crafty than any beast of the field which the LORD God had made. And he said to the woman, "Indeed, has God said, 'You shall not eat from any tree of the garden'?" (Genesis 3:1)

Eve went on to believe the lie of Satan by failing to put faith in God's Word. Satan is no different today as he constantly bombards the believer's mind with a barrage of lies. The Holy Spirit helps us guard against these lies by impressing upon our hearts the truth of God's Word. Many Christians today have been deceived by Satan and have drifted away because of their sins or shortcomings in the faith. They fail to recognize the patience of the Father when His children are willing to turn to Him in repentance. Instead of receiving the Father's love in forgiveness, they believe that God has changed His mind toward them and has abandoned them as His children. The believer becomes despondent, mentally removing himself from the riches of God that have become his possession. This is a crippling lie to the saint who needs to hear the voice of his Father and not the deception of Satan. The Holy Spirit assures us of the unlimited nature of God's grace and love.

Intercession in Prayer

Fifth, the Holy Spirit intercedes for us in our prayer lives. This intercession of the Holy Spirit helps us to pray with a spiritual and eternal perspective according to the will of the Father. Sometimes we are not sure what to pray for, but the Spirit intercedes for our spirit with feelings beyond our comprehension.

*In the same way the Spirit also helps our weakness; for we
do not know how to pray as we should, but the Spirit
Himself intercedes for us with groanings too deep for
words; and He who searches the hearts knows what the
mind of the Spirit is, because He intercedes for the saints
according to the will of God.* (Romans 8:26-27)

I believe this groaning by the Holy Spirit (verse 26) is the cry
for righteousness and complete restoration from the shortcomings of our flesh. As believers, there is always this feeling in our
innermost being to be holy and perfect as the Father is holy and
perfect. This desire of our heart to be more Christ-like begins
with the intercession of the Holy Spirit in prayer with groans that
reflect these desires. Led by the Holy Spirit, the request of our
prayers will be for personal change in order to be more Christ-
like. As the Holy Spirit illuminates truth, causing us to mature,
our minds and hearts will be governed to pray in such a manner.

SUMMARY

God has not only equipped us with all the resources necessary at salvation, but the Son and the Holy Spirit are ministering
on our behalf in order for us to walk in the fullness of our new
standing. Jesus Christ, who made this all possible by His death, is
now interceding for us at the right hand of God. He has provided
us with a privileged position by which we can approach the presence of God with confidence. There are no longer any barriers
that separate us from the Father. Jesus Christ is our High Priest
who identifies with all our weaknesses and temptations, helping
us in our time of need.

The Holy Spirit is also ministering the truths of God's Word,
guiding us in all manners of life and righteousness. He opens our

hearts to discern the wonderful truths of Scripture, leading us away from unrighteousness and guiding us into a life that is God-honoring. Believers are to look to the Holy Spirit in the present reality of their salvation.

The importance of the present role of Jesus Christ and the Holy Spirit needs to be recognized by the believer. Their ministries together, with our new standing before the Father, have provided the believer with more than enough assistance to live in accordance with the abundant life that God has purposed for us.

Chapter Six

THE SPIRITUAL GIFTS

As each one has received a special gift, employ it in serving one another as good stewards of the manifold grace of God. (1 Peter 4:10)

Another product of the believer's salvation are the gifts of the Holy Spirit. These gifts are God-given abilities that equip the saints to serve Him and other Christians in a way that Christ is glorified and believers are edified. These gifts, if used properly in the body of Christ, will encourage and strengthen each believer to be built up in the faith, testifying to the truth of God's Word. There are certain comments and observations that demand our attention before discussing the gifts of the Holy Spirit.

DIFFERENT APPROACHES TO THE GIFTS

First, in the church, the teaching on the gifts of the Holy Spirit has been subject to different interpretations. For example, there are those who believe that certain gifts were confirmatory, that is, they were present during the apostolic age to confirm the truth of the gospel, but are no longer active today. After the foundation of the church was laid, these gifts were no longer needed. This includes the gifts of prophecy, tongues, miracles, and healing. This position is not suggesting that God is not healing or doing miracles today, but that these gifts are not available in individual believers. God heals and performs miracles according to His sovereignty, as well as responding to personal faith and prayer.

Others feel that the completion of the canon, the New Testament, brought an end to the gifts since the believer has everything he needs in the written Word. This position weighs heavily on the word *perfect* in 1 Corinthians 13:10. The word *perfect*, according to the proponents of this position, refers to the completion of the canon. Therefore, the gifts were no longer needed since the canon provided everything necessary for the well-being of the church. This position allows for the leadership gifts like pastor-teacher, but not gifts that are non-essential in the leadership function of the church.

Further differences exist in the way people have interpreted the gifts. For example, the gift of knowledge or tongues and its use varies among different teachers as to how these gifts are characterized in the body of Christ, the church.

This chapter approaches the gifts with the understanding that they are for today, except for one and possibly two (see comments below). The basis for this position is that there is nothing *conclusive* in the Scriptures to dismiss the gifts for today. The objective in this chapter is to be as precise as possible by using the Scriptures and avoiding any speculation or preconceived ideas to the interpretation of the gifts of the Holy Spirit.

GOD'S DESIGN FOR THE BODY OF CHRIST

Second, before addressing the gifts, it is important that we understand how *God has designed the body of Christ, the church.*

In Paul's letter to the Corinthians he addresses this matter and shows how relevant the gifts are to the function of the body of Christ.

For even as the body is one and yet has many members, and all the members of the body, though they are many, are one body, so also is Christ. For by one Spirit we were all baptized into one body, whether Jews or Greeks, whether slaves or free, and we were all made to drink of one Spirit. For the body is not one member, but many. If the foot says, "Because I am not a hand, I am not a part of the body," it is not for this reason any the less a part of the body. And if the ear says, "Because I am not an eye, I am not a part of the body," it is not for this reason any the less a part of the body. If the whole body were an eye, where would the hearing be? If the whole were hearing, where would the sense of smell be? But now God has placed the members, each one of them, in the body, just as He desired. If they were all one member, where would the body be? But now there are many members, but one body. And the eye cannot say to the hand, "I have no need of you"; or again the head to the feet, "I have no need of you." On the contrary, it is much truer that the members of the body which seem to be weaker are necessary; and those members of the body which we deem less honorable, on these we bestow more abundant honor, and our less presentable members become much more presentable, whereas our more presentable members have no need of it. But God has so composed the body, giving more abundant honor to that member which lacked, so that there may be no division in the body, but that the members may have the same care for one another. And if one member suffers,

all the members suffer with it; if one member is honored,
all the members rejoice with it. Now you are Christ's body,
and individually members of it. (1 Corinthians 12:12-27)

In this text, Paul relates the body of Christ to the human body and, in so doing, reveals many pertinent truths. First, there are many members or parts of the body.

For even as the body is one and yet has many members,
and all the members of the body, though they are many,
are one body, so also is Christ. For by one Spirit we were
all baptized into one body, whether Jews or Greeks,
whether slaves or free, and we were all made to drink of
one Spirit. For the body is not one member, but many.
(1 Corinthians 12:12-14)

Every believer has been baptized by the Holy Spirit into the body of Christ at conversion, thereby becoming a member. The reader learns that *members* or *parts of the body*, terms used in this text, are synonymous with gifted people in the body of Christ (cf. 1 Corinthians 12:14, 19-20, 27-28 in the context of 1 Corinthians 12:12-27). Therefore, every believer in the church is a gifted member at the point of conversion when he is baptized into the body of Christ. Apart from the sign gifts such as tongues or prophecy, most gifts will not be as obvious at first. As young believers mature in the faith they will realize what gifts God has given them to function in the body of Christ. This membership of gifted believers in the body is further supported in Romans 12:4-6:

Just as each of us has one body with many members, and
these members do not all have the same function, so in
Christ we who are many form one body, and each member

*belongs to all the others. We have different gifts, according
to the grace given us.* (NIV)

Second, no part or member can ever declare itself independent of the body (verses 15-16).

*If the foot says, "Because I am not a hand, I am not a part
of the body," it is not for this reason any the less a part of
the body. And if the ear says, "Because I am not an eye, I
am not a part of the body," it is not for this reason any the
less a part of the body.* (1 Corinthians 12:15-16)

Each gifted person has to function with the other gifted members of the body. Just as the foot or eye cannot choose to exist independent of the whole human body, a gifted member cannot choose to function apart from the body of Christ.

Third, the body could not be effective if every part were the same.

*If the whole body were an eye, where would the hearing
be? If the whole were hearing, where would the sense of
smell be?* (1 Corinthians 12:17)

If every member had the same gift, where would the body be? If every part of the human body were an eye, it would definitely see well but would cease to be effective in hearing or walking or thinking. If the body of Christ were made up in a way in which everyone had the same gift, how effective would it be? If everyone were a teacher, many other needs in the church would fail to be fulfilled. As the human body cannot operate properly if every part were an eye or an ear, the body of Christ would fail to function properly if every member had the same gift. Therefore, God has provided a diversity of parts or gifted members in order for the body to function properly.

> *But now God has placed the members, each one of them, in the body, just as He desired. If they were all one member, where would the body be? But now there are many members, but one body. And the eye cannot say to the hand, "I have no need of you"; or again the head to the feet, "I have no need of you."* (1 Corinthians 12:18-21)

In the body no part or gifted member can declare another part or gifted member insignificant to the overall function of the body of Christ.

> *On the contrary, it is much truer that the members of the body which seem to be weaker are necessary; and those members of the body which we deem less honorable, on these we bestow more abundant honor, and our less presentable members become much more presentable, whereas our more presentable members have no need of it. But God has so composed the body, giving more abundant honor to that member which lacked, so that there may be no division in the body, but that the members may have the same care for one another.* (1 Corinthians 12:22-25)

All gifts carry the same importance in the proper function of the body. Gifts that appear less significant or less important are just as valuable to the body when it comes to its function. For the church to be effective, every part of the body or member must be given the same care. If one gifted person is neglected in the use of his gift, then the body of Christ as a whole will fail to function in its fullness. This is the meaning behind 1 Corinthians 12:26:

And if one member suffers, all the members suffer with it;
if one member is honored, all the members rejoice with it.

The church as a whole will suffer because God has designed the body of Christ in a way that every gift needs to be flowing in the function of the church. There are gifts that are greater in the body of Christ (see below) but in the function of the church all the gifts are necessary and carry the same importance.

THE NATURE OF THE GIFTS

The third issue that is important to the study of the gifts is our understanding of the nature of the gifts. To begin with, the gifts are given according to the will of the Holy Spirit. Believers do not decide what gifts they will have but rather the Holy Spirit distributes the gifts according to His will.

But one and the same Spirit works all these things, dis-
tributing to each one individually just as He wills. (1 Corinthians 12:11)

God also testifying with them, both by signs and wonders
and by various miracles and by gifts of the Holy Spirit
according to His own will. (Hebrews 2:4)

Second, a gift is not a talent but is divinely endowed to those who are believers. All people have talents but only believers have gifts of the Holy Spirit. Every believer has at least one gift to function in the body of Christ.

But to each one is given the manifestation of the Spirit for
the common good. (1 Corinthians 12:7)

Third, no one gift will be given to everyone and no one believer will have all of the gifts.

For just as we have many members in one body and all the members do not have the same function, so we, who are many, are one body in Christ, and individually members one of another. Since we have gifts that differ according to the grace given to us, each of us is to exercise them accordingly. (Romans 12:4-6a)

Fourth, the gifts are not of equal value—some gifts are greater or more valuable to the church than others.

Now you are Christ's body, and individually members of it. And God has appointed in the church, first apostles, second prophets, third teachers, then miracles, then gifts of healings, helps, administrations, various kinds of tongues. All are not apostles, are they? All are not prophets, are they? All are not teachers, are they? All are not workers of miracles, are they? All do not have gifts of healings, do they? All do not speak with tongues, do they? All do not interpret, do they? But earnestly desire the greater gifts. (1 Corinthians 12:27-31)

The listing from first to last implies from the greater to the lesser. This is reinforced by verse 31, in which Paul tells the believers to desire the greater gifts in the function of the church. A greater gift like pastor-teacher or evangelist in an individual member needs to be operating in the practice of the church. This is not to suggest that the one who has a greater gift is greater than another believer, but his individual gift has more of an impact upon the church members as a whole than someone who has a lesser gift. Therefore, when the church comes together in their meetings it is essential that the greater gifts in individuals are not neglected in the body of Christ. For the most part, the greater gifts find their expression in the leaders (see comments below) of the church. All the gifts need to be flowing for the proper function of the church, but especially the greater gifts in the practice of them (1 Corinthians 12:31; 14:1, 12).

It is important that we understand that the Apostle Paul in verse 31 is not saying for an individual himself to desire greater gifts, which is a common approach by many to this verse. The verse by itself would appear to be saying this, but that interpretation would be inconsistent in numerous ways with the context of 1 Corinthians 12. First, in this passage, Paul is speaking to the body of Christ as a whole. The "you" in verse 27, *"Now you are Christ's body,"* is a collective singular, indicating that he is speaking to the body as a whole and not to individuals. He is basically saying in 1 Corinthians 12:31 and 14:1, where the Apostle Paul continues his thought on the matter, that the greater gifts in individual members are to be operating in their assemblies (see comments above). *Second,* the Holy Spirit decides what gifts we receive when we are baptized into the body of Christ (1 Corinthians 12:11,13). Therefore, we do not decide what gifts we have, but the Holy Spirit, who distributes them according to His will. Our obligation as members is to be faithful to whatever gifts the Holy Spirit has bestowed upon us. *Third,* if Paul were suggesting that we as individual members pursue greater gifts, then he would be contradicting everything he has just said about God's design for the body of Christ. God has given the believers a diversity of gifts (greater and lesser) in order for the church to function harmoniously; therefore, he is admonishing the church to make sure the greater gifts in individual members are flowing. This is further supported by Paul's comments in 1 Corinthians 12:29-30 in which he is presenting rhetorical questions that demand a *no* answer. The text is strongly suggesting that not everyone will have those gifts mentioned in the verses.

> *All are not apostles, are they? All are not prophets, are*
> *they? All are not teachers, are they? All are not workers of*
> *miracles, are they? All do not have gifts of healings, do*
> *they? All do not speak with tongues, do they? All do not*
> *interpret, do they?* (1 Corinthians 12:29-30)

Fourth, when the church is functioning according to the way God has designed it, when every member is being faithful to his gift(s), then it is not necessary for individual members to pursue greater gifts. The church will function properly according to God's design. The diversity of the gifts, greater or lesser, is what brings glory to God as each member serves the body with their individual gift(s).

Fifth, if everyone desired the greater gifts, the lesser gifts would be neglected, causing the body of Christ to be off balance in the way God has designed it. If everyone were a teacher or an evangelist, how would the church address other needs in the body? Remember Paul's words:

> *If the whole body were an eye, where would the hearing*
> *be? If the whole were hearing, where would the sense of*
> *smell be?* (1 Corinthians 12:17)

In returning to the nature of the gifts, the fifth issue to consider is that certain gifts are necessary in order to function in a church office as an elder or deacon. The office or place of service, in itself, is not a gift, but an individual is called to an office within the church to use his gift. It is the responsibility of the church leaders to recognize these gifts in believers in order to train them for leadership.

Sixth, God has purposely designed the body of Christ with a diversity of gifts (see above, God's design for the body); the different gifts promote unity and growth in the church. Therefore, each believer possesses different gifts and the church members depend on each other for personal growth. No one member can function properly, independent of the rest of the body, including those with the greater gifts (1 Corinthians 12:15-16).

Seventh, the purposes of the greater gifts are revealed to us in Ephesians 4:11-13. Although this passage emphasizes the greater gifts that should be operating in leaders, it is appropriate to extend the application of this text to include all the gifts in God's purposes for them.

And He gave some as apostles, and some as prophets, and some as evangelists, and some as pastors and teachers, for the equipping of the saints for the work of service, to the building up of the body of Christ; until we all attain to the unity of the faith, and of the knowledge of the Son of God, to a mature man, to the measure of the stature which belongs to the fullness of Christ. (Ephesians 4:11-13)

Five things are mentioned in these verses: (1) To equip the saints for works of service or ministry; (2) To build up the body of Christ; (3) To help the body attain to the unity of the faith; (4) To grow in the knowledge of Jesus Christ, understanding Him in all His ways; (5) To reach spiritual maturity, becoming like Christ in all His fullness. It is evident how important these greater gifts are to the function of the church.

The text goes on to show the potential results these gifts have upon the saints when exercised appropriately.

As a result, we are no longer to be children, tossed here and there by waves and carried about by every wind of doctrine, by the trickery of men, by craftiness in deceitful scheming; but speaking the truth in love, we are to grow up in all aspects into Him who is the head, even Christ, from whom the whole body, being fitted and held together by what every joint supplies, according to the proper working of each individual part, causes the growth of the body for the building up of itself in love. (Ephesians 4:14-16)

Four things come about as a result: (1) The church reaches maturity in the Word of God; (2) The church maintains the truth in love, in both speech and life; (3) The church makes Christ the source of all of its growth and strength; (4) The church functions harmoniously as each individual does his part.

THE GIFTS OF THE HOLY SPIRIT

With this introduction, we can now discuss the gifts available to the believers in the body of Christ. Three main passages in the New Testament speak about the spiritual gifts: Ephesians 4:11, Romans 12:6-8, and 1 Corinthians 12:4-10. In studying all three, a list can be made showing which gifts are available in the body of Christ.

EPHESIANS 4:11

In the Ephesians passage, as mentioned above, the emphasis is on the greater gifts in leaders. Five gifts are mentioned:

And He gave some as apostles, and some as prophets, and some as evangelists, and some as pastors and teachers. (4:11)

The Gift of Apostleship

The first gift is that of apostleship. An apostle is a divinely appointed representative of God with delegated authority who is commissioned by Christ (cf. Galatians 1:1). The purpose of the gift was to lay the foundation of the church (Ephesians 2:20) and record New Testament revelation as given by the Holy Spirit (Ephesians 3:5).

> *So then you are no longer strangers and aliens, but you are fellow citizens with the saints, and are of God's household, having been built on the foundation of the apostles and prophets, Christ Jesus Himself being the corner stone.*
> (Ephesians 2:19-20)

> *By referring to this, when you read you can understand my insight into the mystery of Christ, which in other generations was not made known to the sons of men, as it has now been revealed to His holy apostles and prophets in the Spirit.* (Ephesians 3:4-5)

The gift was substantiated by the miraculous power that accompanied it (2 Corinthians 12:12; Hebrews 2:3-4; Acts 5:12-16). This miraculous aspect of the gift is what authenticated the truth of the gospel, giving evidence that God was with these apostles in the message they proclaimed. This was necessary because of the resistance and opposition directed at their message in the first century of the church's existence. Those who witnessed these miracles by the apostles had to consider the essence of what they were preaching.

There were certain qualifications for one to function in this gift. It appears from Acts 1:21-22 that the first twelve had to have walked with Jesus during His earthly ministry. Those who had the gift apart from these twelve had to have physically seen the risen Christ. This is the strong implication of 1 Corinthians 9:1, where Paul was defending his apostleship. 1 Corinthians 15:6-7 reveals that five hundred believers who witnessed the resurrection were eligible for this gift. These qualifications would suggest that the gift is not available today. The gift passed into history with the death of the Apostle John around A.D. 95. The purpose of the gift was accomplished by the end of the first century A.D. in laying the foundation of the church and recording New Testament revelation. In the book of Acts, the authority of the apostles is transferred to the elders in the church (cf. Acts 20) since the apostles would not be around much longer.

The Gift of Prophecy

Second, is the gift of prophecy. Those who have this gift receive divine truth from God by direct revelation. This gift along with apostleship was foundational to the church (Ephesians 2:20), and its practice resulted in edification, exhortation, and comfort to the believers (1 Corinthians 14:3-4). In the apostolic age, the use of the term *prophet* was not only applied to anyone who prophesied, but also was associated with someone who held a prominent role in the church and was instrumental in the development of church doctrine and growth. This is strongly suggested in the passage above (Ephesians 4:11), which stresses leadership gifts, as well as Ephesians 2:20, 3:5, and Acts 13:1-3. The prophets, along with the apostles, were revealing New Testament revelation until it was completed. Both gifts were instrumental for laying the foundation of the church (cf. Ephesians 2:19-20). Those who functioned as prophets but were not prominent in church leadership, nonetheless, instructed God's people in spiritual truths by direct revelation. Whatever the content of their message, the gift was used to direct the believers in the ways of God (Acts 15:32; 1 Corinthians 14:3-4) and to predict future events (cf. Acts 21:10-11).

Is prophecy a gift that functions today? Much debate goes on when considering this question in church circles. There are those who feel that with the completion of the New Testament canon this gift is no longer needed. The gift's purpose was reached in laying the foundation of the church (Ephesians 2:19-20) and recording New Testament revelation (Ephesians 3:5). There is no doubt that the complete revelation of God's Word has been made known by the apostles and prophets, but is there a strong scriptural basis for dismissing the gift for today apart from this authoritative role? Many today are proclaiming to be prophets and declaring they are receiving direct revelation from God. Many also have put the church on the defense toward this gift because of the misuse of it by their false proclamations. How are we to approach this issue? Nothing in the Scriptures indicates conclusively that the gift of prophecy is not for today, but as mentioned above, it is safe to say that God is no longer revealing new revelation pertaining to His redemptive plan for man. In that sense there is no longer any need for prophecy in directing us by new revelation—that is, new Scripture. Those who operate and consider themselves prophets in this manner should be looked upon with suspicion. Every self-proclaimed prophet in church history, who has attempted to add new revelation to Scripture, has led people away from the essence of God's redemptive plan for man in the Bible. However, for those who function in this gift apart from declaring new revelation as Scripture, but make proclamations for the edification and comfort of the church, the Scriptures conceivably allow for this function.

In saying that, certain comments demand our attention concerning the practice of prophecy. First, if the gift is for today but is not being used, then perhaps 1 Thessalonians 5:19-20 is being violated: *Do not quench the Spirit; do not despise prophetic utterances.* The church at Thessalonica was hindering this gift from flowing. Paul admonished the believers not to "quench the Spirit" by stopping those with the gift of prophecy.

Second, if the church believes in the gift then perhaps it would be wise to follow the instructions given to us in 1 Corinthians 14 about how the gift should function in a church service.

Let two or three prophets speak, and let the others pass judgment. But if a revelation is made to another who is seated, the first one must keep silent. For you can all prophesy one by one, so that all may learn and all may be exhorted. (1 Corinthians 14:29-31)

Let two or three have the opportunity to express this gift in the service. In saying that, the church today needs to use caution, since many have attempted to infiltrate congregations with their so-called prophetic utterances without ever establishing any creditability among the elders. When a church has determined that a member has the gift, the elders should then provide an environment for the gift to function in the service. With proper preventive measures, the church can safeguard against those who abuse the gift with their false proclamations and allow this greater gift to function in the body of Christ.

Third, in the use of the gift the church needs to look to 1 Corinthians 14:29 where Paul gives instructions when a prophecy is proclaimed: *Let two or three prophets speak, and let the others pass judgment.* The *others* in this passage are those who have the gift of discerning spirits (see below) or mature Christians who can weigh in on the merit of the prophecy. Therefore, the church should have present, when prophecy is being practiced, those who can discern truth from speculation.

Fourth, whether a church is more prominent in this gift than another, the church as a whole must not divide over the use of the gift. There is no doubt the Word of God in its completed form is the greatest tool for guiding us in the will of God. Without diminishing the gift of prophecy, one who studies God's Word intensely and practices it has access to the fullness of truth that was recorded by the Old and New Testament prophets.

The Gift of Evangelism

The gift of evangelism refers to spreading of the gospel by the preaching of the Word. Those who have this gift have an ongoing desire to share Christ with everyone. Their ministry is essential for reaching those outside of the church. The gift should accompany any missionary or church-planting team that is going out to start a new work. The gift is listed with the leadership gifts; therefore, an elder on the church board should have this gift. The elders with this gift encourage the congregation as a whole to continue to reach out to the lost.

The Gift of Pastoring

The gift of pastoring is shepherding the people of God. Those who have this gift have an ongoing desire to minister to the sheep, which is accomplished by feeding the flock with the Word of God and leading by example (1 Peter 5:1-4). A good shepherd nourishes the sheep with good, sound teaching of the Word, applying it in his own life in order to lead by example. Since teaching is essential in his ministry, this gift or *the ability to teach* (cf. 1 Timothy 3:2) is always present in the one who has this gift. He himself will be a good student of the Word in order to supply the congregation with their everyday spiritual needs. The pastor in further fulfilling his role protects the believers from false teachers and doctrines (cf. Acts 20:28-29) and is always encouraging them to continue in the faith.

The Gift of Teaching

The gift of teaching is elaborating the truths of God's Word. Those who have this gift communicate or teach in an organized and understandable way. They have an ongoing desire to study God's Word in order to present it in a proper manner to others. One who has this gift and meets the requirements of an elder (1 Timothy 3:1-7) should be considered to fill that role. As stated earlier, the church must recognize the leadership gifts in young believers and provide an environment in which the gift can be cultivated and grow in the person who possesses it.

ROMANS 12:6-8

In this Romans passage, five additional gifts are added to the list. Prophecy and teaching are also mentioned in this passage, but have already been dealt with.

> *Since we have gifts that differ according to the grace given to us, each of us is to exercise them accordingly: if prophecy, according to the proportion of his faith; if service, in his serving; or he who teaches, in his teaching; or he who exhorts, in his exhortation; he who gives, with liberality; he who leads, with diligence; he who shows mercy, with cheerfulness.* (Romans 12:6-8)

The Gift of Service or Helps

The gift of service is provided to help the body of Christ with physical needs that are necessary in any local church. Those who have this gift have a strong desire to serve wherever they are needed. They are helpful in serving the saints on an individual basis or the church as a whole. Since the deacon is one who serves, it would be advantageous for this gift to be present in the one who holds that office.

The Gift of Exhortation

The gift of exhortation is the ability to encourage people with the spiritual truths of Scripture. One who has this gift gets people excited about the Word and encourages them to act upon it. Usually this gift is correlative with the gifts associated with leadership but is not limited to those roles. Everyone is called to encourage others, but this gift working in an individual has a natural persuasive and uplifting effect upon those around him.

The Gift of Giving

The gift of giving is in the one who gives generously. His heart is open to meeting the financial needs of others in the church. Every believer is obligated to give in his worship of God, but those who have this gift go far beyond the norm in giving. They never feel under compulsion to give and always find joy in this act of benevolence.

The Gift of Ruling

The gift of ruling or leading is the ability to rule in the church, especially organizationally. The gift is probably emphasizing the administrative role in leadership and not so much teaching or shepherding, although they are both associated with this gift. Those who have this gift (with all the other qualifications) should be operating in the office of an elder. They have the ability to orchestrate and organize the business affairs of the church.

The Gift of Mercy

The gift of mercy is expressing compassion towards others. It is showing empathy for the sick and hurting in the body of Christ. There is always a strong sensitivity to those who are in dire need. Those who have this gift are inclined to visit hospitals and rest homes looking to comfort people who are in distress. Their attitude towards the lost, those outside the church, is one of concern and not judgment.

1 CORINTHIANS 12:7-10

The third major passage that speaks of the gifts of the Holy Spirit is 1 Corinthians 12:7-10.

But to each one is given the manifestation of the Spirit for the common good. For to one is given the word of wisdom through the Spirit, and to another the word of knowledge according to the same Spirit; to another faith by the same Spirit, and to another gifts of healing by the one Spirit, and to another the effecting of miracles, and to another prophecy, and to another the distinguishing of spirits, to another various kinds of tongues, and to another the inter- pretation of tongues. (1 Corinthians 12:7-10)

Eight additional gifts that were not mentioned in the previous two passages are added to the list.

The Gift of Wisdom

The gift or word of wisdom is the ability to provide insight upon revealed matters or doctrinal truth. Whereas knowledge of truth provides facts, *the gift of wisdom provides direction in light of knowledge*, drawing out the spiritual implications of what is revealed in God's Word. The one who has this gift can expand on the knowledge of the Scriptures, with spiritual insight making it applicable to a person's needs. Since wisdom is necessary in the church leaders, the gift should be operating in at least one or two of the elders who make up the local church government.

The Gift of Knowledge

The gift or word of knowledge *is the ability to have knowledge of something that is not normally accessible to everyone.* This gift has been given over to different interpretations in the church; that is, this gift is explained or practiced in various ways. In order to safeguard against an unbiblical approach to this gift, we should acknowledge certain issues. First, this gift needs to be distinguished from the gift of prophecy. In prophecy one is receiving direct revelation from God and communicating it to the church. In the gift of knowledge, one is commenting on knowledge he or she has access to, apart from prophecy. Second, those who have this gift have knowledge of something that others in the church do not. This is what distinguishes it as a gift. Third, the word *knowledge,* in the text does not provide us with any insight on what kind of knowledge is being revealed or how it is being revealed. The word speaks of knowledge in general. In saying that, there are many places in Scripture where the word is associated with knowledge of divine truth (cf. 1 Corinthians 1:5; 2 Corinthians 2:14; Romans 11:33). Therefore, it would be wise to limit the context of knowledge to divine things that are edifying to an individual or the church as a whole and not the ability to have knowledge about people that borders on being a psychic.

Differences exist among Bible teachers on how that knowledge is revealed or made accessible to an individual with the gift. There are those who feel that the knowledge comes upon someone at a particular time, in a supernatural way, in which they are able to give another person a word from the Lord. This approach is perhaps suggesting the gift of prophecy (cf. Acts 21:10-11), not so much the gift of knowledge. Others believe the gift expresses itself by one's ability to explain the thoughts of others who had a dream or vision that was incomprehensible to them. An Old Testament example of knowledge coming upon someone in this manner, would be Daniel, when he was able to interpret King Nebuchadnezzar's dream (Daniel 2:26-28). And still others believe the gift manifests itself by one's ability to bring understanding to a situation by way of divine knowledge, God's Word. In this use the person would direct a believer to the Word of God, making it applicable to a person's needs. Whatever one may feel about this gift, remember, the gifts are for building up and edifying the body of Christ (1 Peter 4:10), therefore the gift should only be used in that context.

The Gift of Faith

The gift of faith is the divine ability to trust God in any situation, no matter how bad the circumstances. Whereas, every believer is obligated to live by faith, those who have this gift have an unusual measure of trust in God that goes far beyond the faith exercised by most Christians. All of us are called to persevere and stand firm in the faith, but those who have this gift are able to naturally, stand firm in the midst of the most adverse circumstances without wavering.

The Gift of Healing

The gift of healing is the ability to heal different kinds of illnesses. The plural form of the word *gift* in verse 9 *would suggest that it came upon certain people at certain times and not at random*. When the gift is functioning in a believer, that person by the power of the Holy Spirit becomes an instrument of God to heal the existing illness or sickness in the person.

The Gift of Miracles

The effecting or working of miracles is performing works that are divinely supernatural, beyond the natural laws of science. This gift, along with healing, operated together many times in the book of Acts (cf. Acts 2:22; 8:13). The purpose of the gift is to authenticate the truth of the gospel message by the performance of these miracles. Those who witness miracles are strongly persuaded to believe in what the ministers of God are saying.

The Gift of Discerning Spirits

The gift of discerning spirits is the ability to distinguish what comes from God and what comes from demons or man's lies. It is not so much the aptitude to have insight into human nature but a divine understanding as to the origins of something spoken or claimed by a person in the name of God. That is, one who has this gift can perceive if a person is speaking from God or from some other source. This gift is important in addressing the practice of prophecy in the church. When one prophesies, those who have this gift are able to discern if the message is of God, or demons, or the imagination of the one that is speaking (cf. 1 Corinthians 14:29).

The Gift of Tongues

The gift of tongues is the ability to speak an unknown language that one has not learned (cf. Acts 2:4). It is supernaturally endowed upon a person who speaks a language foreign to his own intellectual ability. The gift personally edifies the member who possesses it—he knows he is speaking a language from God. Acts 2 reveals that the context of the language is praising God. The gift in the book of Acts was instrumental in authenticating the salvation of the Jews and Gentiles.

While Peter was still speaking these words, the Holy Spirit came on all who heard the message. The circumcised believers who had come with Peter were astonished that the gift of the Holy Spirit had been poured out even on the

*Gentiles. For they heard them speaking in tongues and
praising God. Then Peter said, "Can anyone keep these
people from being baptized with water? They have
received the Holy Spirit just as we have."* (Acts 10:44-47 NIV)

The gift of tongues showed the believing Jews that the
Gentiles received the Holy Spirit as a sign of their salvation. This
is why there is a strong emphasis on the gift in conjunction with
the salvation of Jews and Gentiles.

The Gift of Interpretation

The gift of interpretation of tongues gives one the ability to
translate a language one has not learned. This gift leads to the edification of the church (1 Corinthians 14:5). This is true because
others can hear and understand the words of God that were put in
the heart and mind of the one who spoke in tongues.

The Gift of Celibacy

One other gift that is mentioned in 1 Corinthians 7:6-9 is the
gift of celibacy. The one who has this gift is not overcome by the
desires of sexual fulfillment. He or she is content in their single
life and free to serve the Lord without the obligation a spouse or
child would bring. A person who has this gift should consider
remaining single.

THE PROPER PRACTICE OF THE GIFTS IN THE CHURCH

The Holy Spirit has made these gifts available in the body of
Christ. If the gifts are flowing and used properly, the power of
the Holy Spirit will be evident in the church as each member
comes together in one accord, using their individual gifts for the

good of others. In this way the church will uphold its purpose in glorifying God, as each individual remains faithful to his or her gift.

The proper practices of the gifts express themselves in this manner. The apostles and prophets (church leaders) laid the foundation of the church and revealed New Testament revelation. The apostles and prophets still speak today through the direct revelation of God's written Word, the Bible (see other comments above, for a further treatment of these two gifts).

The pastors and teachers use the direct revelation by the apostles and prophets, the Scriptures, in order to nurture and instruct the church in the ways of God. They exhaust their time feeding the sheep through the teaching of the Word and leading by example. The evangelists channel their energy toward the unbelievers by sharing the gospel message, consequently freeing the pastors and teachers to attend to the needs of the congregation. Those with the gift of exhortation get the believers excited about what is being taught and encourage them to persevere in the faith. The elders or pastors who are gifted in ruling or leading attend to the administration and organization of the church, further freeing the teaching pastors to instruct the sheep. These elders use their teaching gift in a secondary role.

The word of wisdom brings wonderful insights upon the teaching of the Word and helps the church leaders make decisions that are necessary in guiding the members. The word of knowledge makes available biblical truths and facts that are necessary at a given time. Those with the gift of service or helps meet the physical needs of the church in order to allow the elders to apply themselves to leadership matters. Those with the gift of mercy set an example to the church by being sensitive to the hurting and sick. They also lighten the burden of the leadership by making themselves available to visit the sick and hurting. The gift of discerning spirits protects the church from false prophecies and the infiltration of false teachers. Those who have the gift of faith encourage the believers to trust in God no matter how bad circumstances appear. The one with the gift of giving encourages fellow believers to give freely.

The gifts of healing and miracles testify to the truth of God's Word and increase the faith of God's people. The gift of tongues edifies the individual who has it and its interpretation edifies the church (1 Corinthians 14:5). The gift of celibacy allows one to devote himself fully to God without the responsibility a spouse or family brings. All of the gifts are to be practiced in the context of God's love (1 Corinthians 13).

THE BENEFITS OF THE GIFTS TO ONE ANOTHER

When each believer is faithful in exercising the gifts they have been entrusted with, the church as a whole will be built up, growing in the grace and knowledge of our Lord Jesus Christ (cf. Ephesians 4:11-13). When each member exercises their individual gifts, the body matures as the believers in their fellowship glean wonderful insight from each other. For example, many have become fine teachers of the Bible without the gift of teaching because they were good students of the Word, taught by those who had the gift of teaching. Many have grown abundantly in the wisdom and mercy of God without these gifts because they gleaned from the example of others who possess the gift of wisdom and mercy. The rule is this: whether one has certain gifts or not, a person who is functioning in the body of Christ will mature in areas where he was not necessarily gifted. He will display qualities that resemble the gifts by maturing in the faith. In so doing, the purpose of the body, in the way that God has designed it (1 Corinthians 12:12-27; Romans 12:4-8), will be accomplished and Jesus Christ will be glorified.

FELLOWSHIP AND THE GIFTS

From the comments above, we see how important it is that an individual always be in fellowship. This is because first, he or she has a gift for the rest of the body. When a believer is out of fellowship, that person is robbing the church of the gift he possesses. Remember, God has designed the body of Christ in a unique way in which all the gifts are necessary for its proper function. Second, each member of the church needs to have access to the other gifts of the body in order to mature. Therefore, those who are not functioning in the church are depriving themselves of the gifts that are essential to their spiritual well-being and growth.

POINT OF INTEREST

One final noteworthy thought is the distinction between the gifts and spiritual blessings. The purpose of our gifts is to bring glory to God by serving one another with these spiritual abilities, growing and maturing together in the grace of God (see above). In saying that, God is not limited in bestowing spiritual blessings upon His children apart from the gifts. Whether believers have certain gifts or not, a member in the body of Christ can still be blessed at a particular time with certain qualities that resemble the gifts, such as wisdom, mercy, faith, healing, performing miracles, etc. God is sovereign over all things; therefore, He blesses His children with divine qualities by responding to the personal prayers and personal faith of His people. He honors the request of those who call on Him for wisdom, faith, and whatever other qualities are needed in times of need. This is not to suggest that a certain gift becomes his possession at that time. The Holy Spirit has determined our gifts at salvation, but the believer by way of answered prayer has received certain abilities at a particular time. The difference, in contrast to a gifted member, is that those who possess certain abilities by their gifts will naturally function in these ways, whereas the one without these gifts will temporarily function in this manner by way of answered prayer to his personal faith.

One may ask then, why the gifts, if God answers prayer in this manner. Remember, in God's design for the body of Christ, the gifts are unique and intrumental in the proper function of the church. Each member is dependent on one another's gifts to grow and mature in the faith; in effect, bringing glory to God, as we serve one another with these spiritual abilities.

SUMMARY

God has designed the body of Christ in a way in which every gift is significant to the overall function of the church. In order to uphold the value of the gifts, one must understand certain issues pertaining to the gifts of the Holy Spirit. First, the gifts are to function in accordance with God's design for the body of Christ. Second, the nature of the gifts must be understood in order to apply them properly. Third, every member should know what gifts they possess. Fourth, the gifts should be practiced in the proper manner in the church. The leaders would do well in pointing these things out to the congregation when it comes to the spiritual gifts in the local church.

Chapter Seven

THE OBLIGATION OF THE BELIEVER TO HIS CALLING

Therefore, I urge you, brothers, in view of God's mercy, to offer your bodies as living sacrifices, holy and pleasing to God—this is your spiritual act of worship. Do not conform any longer to the pattern of this world, but be transformed by the renewing of your mind. Then you will be able to test and approve what God's will is—his good, pleasing and perfect will. (Romans 12:1-2 NIV)

How should the believer respond to God's gift of salvation? The above passage of Romans follows eleven chapters of theological teaching in relationship to God's plan of salvation. Paul begins with the admonishment, *Therefore I urge you, brothers, in view of God's mercy.* In light of everything God has done by His mercy and grace in the believer's calling, Paul is ready to give the believers practical instructions for godly living.

THE DEDICATED LIFE

Romans 12:1-2 is foundational to fulfilling our obligation to our calling. It admonishes the believer to present his body as a living and holy sacrifice to God. It requires the complete dedication of our lives to fulfill the purpose of our calling. Every part of our being is to be set apart for the work of God. We are to give up our rights and desires of our flesh, submitting to the ways of God in all righteousness, becoming an effective witness for the gospel message. The above text indicates two things the believer must do to lay a foundation for godly living. First, he must separate himself from the world system or mentality (*do not be conformed to this world* verse 2). That is, to come out from it, no longer loving the things of the world that oppose the truth of Christ and stimulate our fleshly desires. The Apostle John said it best in his epistle.

> *Do not love the world nor the things in the world. If anyone loves the world, the love of the Father is not in him. For all that is in the world, the lust of the flesh and the lust of the eyes and the boastful pride of life, is not from the Father, but is from the world. The world is passing away, and also its lusts; but the one who does the will of God lives forever.* (1 John 2:15-17)

The text in 1 John is not saying for the believer to leave this world to escape its corruption, but he is not to be contaminated by the ungodliness surrounding him. He is to abstain from anything that has the appearance of evil or opposes the things of God. He is not to make any provisions for the flesh (Romans 13:14) that would put him in a compromising position that might trigger his sinful tendencies. A believer who loves God more than his own life will not compromise his faith or allow his relationship with God to be hindered. He will at all times live to please God, concerned with how his actions affect his relationship to the Father.

The second thing we do in presenting our bodies to God is allow our minds to be transformed by the renewing of the Holy Scriptures (*but be transformed by the renewing of your mind* verse 2). The Scriptures edify and strengthen us by directing us in the path of God. They enable one to discern between good and evil, truth and deception, righteousness and ungodliness. God's Word is living and active.

> *For the word of God is living and active and sharper than any two-edged sword, and piercing as far as the division of soul and spirit, of both joints and marrow, and able to judge the thoughts and intentions of the heart.* (Hebrews 4:12)

The Word reveals the secrets and motives of our hearts that are sometimes ungodly. Our hearts are laid bare before God through His Word, which convicts us of any deception or sin in our hearts. It is so powerful that when we submit to the Word in obedience and humility, it pierces our hearts with the truth of righteousness. The Scriptures are the means that the Holy Spirit uses to bring change and direction to our Christian lives. When we turn to God in obedience, the Holy Spirit impresses upon our minds and hearts the need for change and guides us in the direction of righteousness. As we submit to the leading of the Holy Spirit, the fullness of God's grace becomes available, uprooting our shortcomings and resulting in godliness in our deeds and thoughts.

THE FULLNESS OF THE HOLY SPIRIT, THE SPIRIT-LED LIFE

When the believer has once and for all presented his body to the work of God, he is able to understand the ways of God and His perfect will (*so that you may prove what the will of God is, that which is good and acceptable and perfect* verse 2). He is now in a position to live in the fullness of the Holy Spirit, which is the *second* obligation of the believer in the purpose of his calling.

> *And do not get drunk with wine, for that is dissipation, but be filled with the Spirit.* (Ephesians 5:18)

In positional truth (our new standing), the Holy Spirit has all of us. In this command, the emphasis is on the believer to have all of the Holy Spirit that indwells him. This command requires the believer to be totally submissive to the Holy Spirit in his daily life—to be controlled and led by the Spirit in all matters of life. The believer who is submissive will continue to grow in the grace of God as the Holy Spirit leads him. This command, to "be filled with the Spirit," is imperative for the believer to mature in the Christian faith. It is not an option, but the obligation of every believer in his obedience to God.

The tense in the verb "be filled" implies a repetitive action in which the believer is to go on to continuous fillings of the Holy Spirit. Whatever our deficiencies or wherever we are in our Christian walk, we should constantly look to be filled or controlled by the Spirit as God leads us, one step at a time, in the maturing process. The Father, through the Holy Spirit, continues to reveal areas in our lives in which we need to grow. A Spirit-led life will help us to respond in the proper way.

The Evidence of the Spirit-Filled Life

A believer who is maturing by being Spirit-led expresses himself in this manner: first, he is obedient to the Word of God. There is no way a believer is living a Spirit-filled life if he has a disregard for the Scriptures that command him to live in a godly way. Many people today have substituted emotionalism for obedience as the evidence of a Spirit-filled life. The outward manners and actions (dancing and shouting) of the person become the criteria for his spirituality instead of the inward change in obedience that needs to take place in his heart. It is impossible to walk in the fullness of the Holy Spirit without obedience to the Word of God. This first issue in many ways defines a Spirit-filled life.

Second, the believer is always growing and conforming to the image of Jesus Christ.

The one who says he abides in Him [Jesus] ought himself to walk in the same manner as He walked. (1 John 2:6)

This second item takes us beyond the necessary obedience to God's Word. To walk in the same manner as Jesus walked is to be totally consumed with the same desires and will that Christ had in His love for the Father. In the same way, the believer is driven by a desire to be more Christ-like, which includes a desire to please the Father in all His ways. Believers must have the mind of Christ in everything they do today. Our will must be caught up in the will of the Father, our desires must be in harmony with the Father's desires, and our conduct must follow a path according to the ways of the Father.

We are not only sensitive to sin, but also to anything that might be unbecoming in our walk with God. When the Holy Spirit is constantly leading us in this manner, our relationship with God will be more than just following His commandments. It will include a facet of our life that is always looking to be a witness for God and bring glory to His name.

The third evidence of a Spirit-filled life is endurance through the tough times in life. The believer perseveres through the hardships and tribulations of life, knowing that this is the will of God.

He is aware of the fact that his circumstances play a role in building his character and shaping him into the image of the Son. The Spirit-led believer considers the spiritual implications of his situation despite the discomfort it brings to him. Instead of fleeing from these God-given trials, he sees the need to persevere, knowing that God is using his circumstances to build him up in the faith. This was James' admonishment to the believers.

> *Consider it all joy, my brethren, when you encounter various trials, knowing that the testing of your faith produces endurance. And let endurance have its perfect result, so that you may be perfect and complete, lacking in nothing.*
> (James 1:2-4)

Fourth, the believer who is Spirit-filled has a strong awareness of how his actions affect the gospel message and others. He is concerned about his conduct, not wishing to put any stumbling blocks in the path of his hearers. This was the desire of the Apostle Paul who submitted himself to the conscience of all men without compromising before God, in order to gain a hearing for the gospel message.

> *For though I am free from all men, I have made myself a slave to all, so that I may win more. To the Jews I became as a Jew, so that I might win Jews; to those who are under the Law, as under the Law though not being myself under the Law, so that I might win those who are under the Law; to those who are without law, as without law, though not being without the law of God but under the law of Christ, so that I might win those who are without law. To the weak I became weak, that I might win the weak; I have become all things to all men, so that I may by all means*

save some. I do all things for the sake of the gospel, so that
I may become a fellow partaker of it. (1 Corinthians 9:19-23)

What a wonderful testimony of a man who loved God and was Spirit-led. The only thing that mattered to Paul was that people would come to the saving knowledge of Jesus Christ through his witness for God. In his Spirit-led life this one thing always motivated Paul. He did everything out of love for the glory of God.

Whether, then, you eat or drink or whatever you do, do all
to the glory of God. Give no offense either to Jews or to
Greeks or to the church of God; just as I also please all men
in all things, not seeking my own profit but the profit of the
many, so that they may be saved. (1 Corinthians 10:31-33)

As believers we should echo these same words in our own lives, walking in a manner that glorifies God and always motivated by our desire to please Him. When this is true in our lives, the fruit of our faith pours out of us, making a huge impact for the kingdom of God in the lives of those around us. All this is possible in a Spirit-filled life. Remember, this is not an option but a command from our Father in heaven.

This kind of commitment to the faith is accompanied by the following characteristics: thankfulness, joy, and peace in the Holy Spirit.

Rejoice always; pray without ceasing; **in everything give**
thanks*; for this is God's will for you in Christ Jesus.*
(1 Thessalonians 5:16-18, emphasis added)

For the kingdom of God is not eating and drinking, **but**
righteousness and peace and joy *in the Holy Spirit.*
(Romans 14:17, emphasis added)

As we rest in God by practicing righteousness, we become content in every situation or circumstance, knowing the Father loves us and is watching over us. Instead of grumbling and complaining in our hardships, we find a place in our hearts to give thanks to God as the joy and peace of our salvation remains intact.

The Fruit of a Spirit-Filled Life

The final product of a mature Christian, who constantly goes on to subsequent fillings of the Spirit, is a holy and blameless life, separated from evil and above reproach. He is sensitive to ungodliness, not wanting to identify with anything that is unbecoming for a Christian. He is pure in heart in that his motives are innocent and absent of any evil intentions. He is humble and gracious, not considering himself better than others. There is gentleness with people, never allowing for rudeness or harshness in relating to them. He is kind to others and always considers their needs. The believer has empathy for people, showing compassion and mercy in times of need. He is patient, understanding, and considerate toward shortcomings in others, with a genuine love for them. This love which is the basis for all his actions, is unconditional and self-sacrificing in nature (cf. Romans 12:9).

COMMITMENT TO FELLOWSHIP

In order for these godly attributes to be reinforced, the believer must devote himself to the fellowship of believers provided by God in the body of Christ. This is the **third** obligation to his calling in Christ.

Let us hold fast the confession of our hope without wavering, for He who promised is faithful; and let us consider how to stimulate one another to love and good deeds, not forsaking our own assembling together, as is the habit of some, but encouraging one another; and all the more as you see the day drawing near. (Hebrews 10:23-25)

The passage above shows how we are to stimulate or provoke one another to love and good deeds. This only happens when we are in fellowship with our brothers and sisters in the body of Christ. The encouragement we need to persevere is found in fellowship with other godly Christians. There is no such thing as the lone Christian. Those who insist on believing they can live independent of the church are depriving themselves of the support they need to go on to the fullness of the Christian faith.

The Essential Practices of Fellowship

There are four things that should be practiced in the local church to enhance fellowship. In the book of Acts we are given insight into these pertinent practices.

They were continually devoting themselves to the apostles' teaching and to fellowship, to the breaking of bread and to prayer. (Acts 2:42)

These four items are the teaching of the Word, fellowship, the breaking of bread (perhaps a reference to the fellowship meal practiced by the early church, followed by the Lord's supper) and prayer. All four practices were the heart of the first-century church. Churches today should follow the same path in their fellowship. The teaching of the Word protects us from the deceitfulness of sin. The fellowship of believers is a safeguard against the attacks of the enemy. The breaking of bread reminds us of our common goal and purpose as believers. Prayer is the means by which we communicate with the Father in an intimate way. If the leaders are promoting these items in the church functions, the believers will have a healthy spiritual diet in their assemblies. It is quite amazing how churches today have substituted many other practices to get people involved in their Christian walk. There is a place for other practices in the church, as long as they do not replace or diminish these essential items for maturity.

THE DISCIPLINE OF THE FAITH

One final issue that cannot afford to go unnoticed is the *discipline of the faith*. This is brought out in 1 Corinthians 9:24-27:

> *Do you not know that in a race all the runners run, but only one gets the prize? Run in such a way as to get the prize. Everyone who competes in the games goes into strict training. They do it to get a crown that will not last; but we do it to get a crown that will last forever. Therefore I do not run like a man running aimlessly; I do not fight like a man beating the air. No, I beat my body and make it my slave so that after I have preached to others, I myself will not be disqualified for the prize.* (NIV)

Believers, to live in the fullness of the Christian faith, demands discipline on their part. The Apostle Paul above speaks about beating his body into submission—the discipline necessary to fulfill his calling to the obedience of the faith. Paul knew that the body demands its freedom and rights to express itself according to the sinful ways of the fallen nature, which in reality is a self-centered life. A self-centered life will disregard what God is trying to accomplish in us as His instruments of righteousness. This cannot be. Although we are totally set free by the born-again experience (positional truth), the tendencies of the flesh are still active in us. We as believers play an active role, through discipline, in the sanctifying process of the Holy Spirit. It is not as if we are robots who have no control over our choices, but in the freedom we have in Christ, we discipline our bodies in order to serve God, with all our being. To be led by the Holy Spirit includes the discipline of the faith, gaining control over the flesh as we work in harmony with the sanctifying ministry of the Holy Spirit.

SUMMARY

As believers we have an obligation and a responsibility to our calling in Christ. We are to dedicate our lives to the work of God by presenting our bodies as an offering in our service to Him. We are to separate ourselves from the world system and renew our minds and hearts by the guidance of the Scriptures that direct us in the ways and will of God. We are commanded by God to be led and guided by the Holy Spirit in every aspect of our lives. The Spirit-led life is measured in four ways: total obedience, conforming to the person of Jesus Christ, enduring hardships and trials, and being a witness to the gospel message. We are to protect against spiritual laziness and press on in our Christian walk by disciplining our bodies in the faith, always looking to grow in the grace of God. We are to be devoted to the fellowship of believers, encouraging each other and spurring one another on toward good deeds in the faith. The result of this is a love and a righteousness that reflects the unconditional love and holiness of God. This fulfills the purpose of our calling to be holy and blameless as children of God (Ephesians 1:4).

Chapter Eight

Spiritual Warfare

*Finally, be strong in the Lord and in the strength of His might.
Put on the full armor of God, so that you will be able to stand
firm against the schemes of the devil. For our struggle is not
against flesh and blood, but against the rulers, against the powers,
against the world forces of this darkness, against the spiritual
forces of wickedness in the heavenly places.* (Ephesians 6:10-12)

The Real Enemy

The believer's struggle in spiritual warfare is not against flesh
and blood, but against the demonic forces of evil that have as
their head the father of lies, the devil. He is called the prince of this
world (John 12:31) and the god of this age (2 Corinthians 4:4), who
has as his subjects all those who are outside the body of Christ, the
non-believers (cf. 1 John 5:19; Ephesians 2:1-2). The leading advo-
cates of his false kingdom are the spiritual forces of wickedness
(Ephesians 6:12), and the false apostles (2 Corinthians 11:13-15),
teachers, and prophets (2 Peter 2:1-3; Matthew 13:37-39). Satan,
whose ultimate demise is prophesied in the book of Revelation, is

not giving up without a fight. He is someone who cannot be dismissed as a fictional character, but is a real being attested to by Old and New Testament writings. He has a purpose for his existence and has set up a counter-kingdom in order to thwart the plans of God for His people. Satan is trying to deceive and destroy the truth of the gospel message by attempting to bring down the children of God who make up the pillar of truth, the church (1 Timothy 3:15).

THE WEAPONS OF SATAN

The means by which Satan attempts to destroy the church are varied. The *first* is persecution. This is implied in Peter's epistle in which he describes Satan as a roaring lion ready to devour anyone who is vulnerable.

> *Be of sober spirit, be on the alert. Your adversary, the devil, prowls around like a roaring lion, seeking someone to devour. But resist him, firm in your faith, knowing that the same experiences of suffering are being accomplished by your brethren who are in the world.* (1 Peter 5:8-9)

Persecution

The first three hundred years of church history are saturated with persecution directed at God's people. This was Satan's primary means at that time to snuff out the message of the cross. The saints were persecuted for their faith, resulting in loss of property, physical harm, and even death. These attacks by Satan did not prevail against the work of God in the church. This was the promise of Jesus in Matthew.

> *I also say to you that you are Peter, and upon this rock I will build My church; and the gates of Hades will not overpower it.* (Matthew 16:18)

The gates of Hades is a Jewish idiom for death. Death will not put an end to the existence or perpetuation of the church. They crucified Jesus, they crucified the apostles, they have martyred the faithful saints throughout the Church Age to our present day, but the church is still standing and testifying to the truth of Jesus Christ. It has always appeared to the enemies of God that there was immediate victory through persecution, but this supposed victory by Satan was only a temporary setback for the church saints.

False Teaching

In many places, as in the United States, Satan is not using the primary weapon of persecution, since the government protects us, but has infiltrated the church with damaging doctrine that has destroyed the integrity of the local church. This is the *second* means by which he attempts to thwart the plans of God for His people. Regrettably, he has had great success in fusing his diabolical ideas into the doctrine of the church. This second tool of the enemy is the one that has destroyed many churches throughout history without doing any physical harm to the saints. It is subtle and deceptive, often going unnoticed by the congregation. This is why Jesus constantly warned the disciples to guard against false teachers, who are the pawns of Satan in carrying out his diabolical lies. In Matthew 13, Jesus told the parable of the wheat and tares to demonstrate to the disciples how Satan is sowing his seed in the Present Kingdom Age.

Jesus presented another parable to them, saying, "The kingdom of heaven may be compared to a man who sowed good seed in his field. But while his men were sleeping, his enemy came and sowed tares among the wheat, and went away. But when the wheat sprouted and bore grain, then the tares became evident also. The slaves of the landowner came and said to him, 'Sir, did you not sow good seed in your field? How then does it have tares?' And he said to them, 'An enemy has done this!' The slaves said to him, 'Do you want us, then, to go and gather them up?' But he said, 'No; for while you are gathering up the tares, you may uproot the wheat with them. Allow both to grow together until the harvest; and in the time of the harvest I will say to the reapers, "First gather up the tares and bind them in bundles to burn them up; but gather the wheat into my barn." (Matthew 13:24-30)

The meaning of the parable is given in verses 36-43:

Then He left the crowds and went into the house. And His disciples came to Him and said, "Explain to us the parable of the tares of the field." And He said, "The one who sows the good seed is the Son of Man, and the field is the world; and as for the good seed, these are the sons of the kingdom; and the tares are the sons of the evil one; and the enemy who sowed them is the devil, and the harvest is the end of the age; and the reapers are angels. So just as the tares are gathered up and burned with fire, so shall it be at the end of the age. The Son of Man will send forth His angels, and they will gather out of His kingdom all stumbling blocks, and those who commit lawlessness, and will throw them into the furnace of fire; in that place there will be weeping and gnashing of teeth. Then THE RIGHTEOUS WILL SHINE FORTH AS THE SUN in the kingdom of their Father. He who has ears, let him hear." (Matthew 13:36-43)

Highlighting the major points of the parable, one can say that as Christ is sowing good seed in the hearts of man, Satan is sowing bad seed through false teachers. The wheat and tares appear to resemble each other until the wheat sprouts, revealing the tares growing up alongside them. At the early stages of growth there is a strong similarity between the wheat and tares. This indicates in the parable that the false teachers of Satan will not easily be detected because of the huge deception that hides their false message. This is because the false teachers use the Word of God in their preaching, distorting it to their own purposes (cf. 2 Peter 3:16). The parable tells us these false teachers will be with us to the end of the age (cf. Matthew 13:27-30, 37-42).

The reality of false teachers is further developed in the epistles of the New Testament.

For such men are false apostles, deceitful workers, disguising themselves as apostles of Christ. No wonder, for even Satan disguises himself as an angel of light. Therefore it is not surprising if his servants also disguise themselves as servants of righteousness, whose end will be according to their deeds. (2 Corinthians 11:13-15)

The emphasis in this passage is on their ability to disguise themselves as servants of God, taking on a form of godliness. Their appearance of truth is only an illusion, hiding their false message under religious pretenses.

In Peter's second epistle, the content of their lying message is revealed.

But false prophets also arose among the people, just as there will also be false teachers among you, who will secretly introduce destructive heresies, even denying the

Master who bought them, bringing swift destruction upon
themselves. Many will follow their sensuality, and because
of them the way of the truth will be maligned; and in their
greed they will exploit you with false words; their judg-
ment from long ago is not idle, and their destruction is not
asleep. (2 Peter 2:1-3)

Three facts are mentioned in this passage about their teaching. First, they introduce destructive heresies (verse 1). They
teach other means of salvation apart from faith in Jesus Christ. In
the nineteenth and twentieth centuries, we have seen the rise of
many cults. None of them uphold the teaching of the Bible of salvation by faith alone. All of them have introduced works as a
means of salvation.

Second, they deny the Master (verse 1) that bought them,
bringing themselves swift destruction. One common ingredient
that runs throughout their false message is the failure to recognize the deity of Jesus Christ. Christ is demoted in their doctrine
to someone less than God. Their teachings include Christ, but
they fail to recognize His deity, denying the sovereignty of the
Lord in the message of salvation. Jesus has a secondary role in
their religion.

Third, the way of truth is maligned (verse 2). The teaching of
the Word is distorted and hindered because of their unregenerate
minds. The man without the Spirit cannot discern the spiritual
implications of God's Word (cf. 1 Corinthians 2:6-16). This
maligning of God's Word includes stories they have made up
(verse 3) with no biblical foundation to support them.

The Apostle Paul, in his farewell address to the Ephesian elders, reminded them of the real danger of false teachers, who
would rise up in their own congregations.

Be on guard for yourselves and for all the flock, among which the Holy Spirit has made you overseers, to shepherd the church of God which He purchased with His own blood. "I know that after my departure savage wolves will come in among you, not sparing the flock; and from among your own selves men will arise, speaking perverse things, to draw away the disciples after them." (Acts 20:28-30)

Paul reveals in writing to Timothy that their message is the work of demons who are introducing these lying doctrines into the church. The false teachers are the ones who promote their lies to the church disguised as truth.

The Spirit clearly says that in later times some will abandon the faith and follow deceiving spirits and things taught by demons. Such teachings come through hypocritical liars, whose consciences have been seared as with a hot iron. (1 Timothy 4:1-2 NIV)

Temptation and Doubt

The *third* means by which Satan is attempting to hinder the church is by his personal attacks on the saints. This is accomplished in two ways, tempting the believers to sin and bringing fear upon their lives. It is always Satan's intention to draw the believer away from God, by either appealing to him through his sinful nature or bringing doubt into his life. These are ongoing tactics of his that we as believers need to be ready for. If the believer is not prepared, then he or she will fall prey to the schemes of the enemy. Many believers today are failing to have victory in their Christian lives due to their failure to combat Satan's relentless attacks upon their minds. He is persistently bombarding us with ideas that distract from the promises of God in His Word. He is bringing fear and doubt along with temptation that feeds our flesh. When he has blinded us from the victory we have in Christ and misrepresented the Father's love for us, then he has gained a stronghold in our minds and hearts. He tempted Eve in the Garden of Eden (Genesis 3:1-4) by putting doubt in her mind and getting her to question the things that God had revealed. It is not any different today. He is using the very same methods he used to introduce sin into God's kingdom on earth.

Causing Division

The *fourth* means by which he comes against the church is to bring division among God's people. Not to give Satan more credit than is due him, but perhaps he did learn one truth from Jesus Christ—a house divided against itself cannot survive.

> *And knowing their thoughts Jesus said to them, "Any kingdom divided against itself is laid waste; and any city or house divided against itself will not stand. "If Satan casts out Satan, he is divided against himself; how then will his kingdom stand?* (Matthew 12:25-26)

By causing division among the brethren he has disrupted the unity of the church, which is essential for maintaining its common goal, in bringing glory to God in our love for one another. In many good, sound churches today where the Word of God is being taught and the church is protected from persecution, Satan has opted to use this device in order to bring about his destructive purpose. He has often succeeded, as church history since the Protestant Reformation, verifies.

THE BELIEVER'S DEFENSE:
THE FULL ARMOR OF GOD

We have an enemy who's working overtime. How are we to engage in this kind of spiritual warfare to combat Satan in his attempts to cripple the saints and the church of its intended purpose? The Apostle Paul gives us a huge part of the answer in the book of Ephesians: *Put on the full armor of God.*

> *Therefore put on the full armor of God, so that when the day of evil comes, you may be able to stand your ground, and after you have done everything, to stand. Stand firm then, with the belt of truth buckled around your waist, with the breastplate of righteousness in place, and with your feet fitted with the readiness that comes from the gospel of peace. In addition to all this, take up the shield of faith, with which you can extinguish all the flaming arrows of the evil one. Take the helmet of salvation and the sword of the Spirit, which is the word of God.* (Ephesians 6:13-17 NIV)

The Belt of Truth

Six pieces of armor are mentioned in this text. All six are necessary to deflect the flaming darts of the enemy in his diabolical campaign against the believers in Christ. The first, the *belt of truth,* is foundational to the other five. Without truth it is impossible to live a godly life and move forward in faith against the lies of the enemy. The Word of God is the embodiment of truth in written form. It is the spiritual barometer that tests all things in accordance with God's revealed will. It allows us to know what is from God and what is from the ideas of men who carry out the teachings of Satan. Through divine revelation, the wisdom of God, one understands the depths of the Father's heavenly knowledge that gives us meaning, guidance, and direction in this life. Jesus Christ and His Word is the revelation of truth. Christ, in His humanity and His teaching, has revealed the fullness of the Father in all His holiness and wisdom (cf. John 14:6-7). To the believer, this is the basis for what he believes and for godly living. Everything else that is not of truth is of the devil. Man is carrying out the deception of Satan. He has continuously tried to suppress the truth of God by burying it under a pile of philosophies and humanistic ideas that hide the reality of God and His Word. The believer, who has cultivated his relationship with Christ, protects himself against these lies and becomes a rock that cannot be moved by the schemes of Satan. The belt of truth—put it on.

The Breastplate of Righteousness

The second piece of armor is the *breastplate of righteousness.* This is the practice of holiness in which we conduct ourselves in the righteousness of Christ. The believer who puts on this piece of the armor is living a Spirit-filled life and growing in the richness of God's grace. In spiritual warfare, it is the piece of armor that protects the church against disunity. The fruit of righteousness is love. The believer who has matured in righteousness expresses the essence of love in every aspect of his life. He will not only walk in a manner that is pleasing to God, but in humility and love; he has a genuine concern for others. This Christ-centered attitude toward others protects against division in the body of Christ caused by self-centeredness and immaturity. Let us maintain the unity of the Spirit by putting on the breastplate of righteousness.

The Gospel of Peace

The third piece of armor is the *gospel of peace.* This is peace in the believer's heart because of the assurance he has in knowing that God is in control of his life. The opposite of peace is fear. Fear is an element used by the enemy to stall the forward progress of the believer. Many have shipwrecked their walk with God by giving in to their fears. The gospel of peace, the peace of God, gives us solid footing against the fear of the enemy. Instead of shying away from trials and persecution, God's peace helps us to persevere through these adverse conditions. The believer walks through hard times feeling the presence of God who comforts him with the inexpressible joy and peace that come from knowing God's love. The gospel of peace leaves no place for fear.

The Shield of Faith

The fourth piece of armor is the *shield of faith*. This protects us against unbelief. The enemy, as we have learned, is always attempting to bring doubt into our minds. When one's faith in God is slipping or shattered, it will not be long before his spiritual life begins to decline. When we exercise faith in our lives, we are protected from the barrage of arrows intended to snuff out the truth of God. Our faith in God needs to keep growing. This happens as we experience the goodness of God by practicing and trusting in His Word. The shield of faith instills in us the absolute certainty of God's promises, turning away Satan's arrows of unbelief.

The Helmet of Salvation

The fifth piece of armor is the *helmet of salvation*. We learn from 1 Thessalonians 5:8 that the helmet represents the hope we have in Christ. Hope is a strong and powerful motivation in the Christian life. Without hope, the believer is left with emptiness in the midst of all the riches he possesses in Christ. This life offers many difficulties by way of hardship and trials but none more devastating than a life without hope. You can take away a believer's money and he will survive. You can take away his spouse and he will survive. You can even take away a limb and he will survive, but if you take away his hope in Christ you have crippled him in an enormous way. Satan knows this; therefore, his plan is to distract the believer from an eternal perspective of life. The believer, who holds on to the things of this world too tightly, helps Satan in his plan. When that happens, the believer ends up putting his hope in temporary things that are here today and gone tomorrow.

Now understand why Peter encouraged the believers to completely set their minds on the hope they have in Jesus Christ.

> *Therefore, prepare your minds for action, keep sober in spirit, fix your hope completely on the grace to be brought to you at the revelation of Jesus Christ.* (1 Peter 1:13)

The believer needs to cultivate this hope. He needs to have an eternal perspective to life in order to look beyond this life's obstacles and the temporary nature of material things. The problems and issues of everyday life fade in comparison to the glory that will be revealed in us at the coming of Jesus Christ for His church (cf. Romans 8:18). The inheritance that we have waiting for us in our heavenly calling should be more than enough to bring satisfaction and contentment in our new lives in Christ.

The Sword of the Spirit

The sixth piece of armor is the *sword of the Spirit*, the Word of God. In relation to spiritual warfare, it is the piece of armor that protects us against the temptations of Satan. It provides us with an offensive capability in our battle with the enemy. It is interesting to note that Jesus used the Word of God to fight back against the temptations of Satan (Matthew 4:4,7,10). If this was Jesus' primary defense against temptation in His humanity, then we would do well following His example. When we hide the Word of God in our hearts, it becomes a valuable tool in protecting against the temptations of the evil one in baiting our sinful nature. Fight back temptation with the Word of God.

THE SPECIAL PRIVILEGE OF PRAYER

Paul ends this passage with the admonishment to the saints to pray on all occasions.

And pray in the Spirit on all occasions with all kinds of prayers and requests. With this in mind, be alert and always keep on praying for all the saints (Ephesians 6:18 NIV)

Prayer is a mighty tool in the hand of the believer who trusts in God for all his needs. God honors the prayers of those who come to Him in faith. He hears our cries in the midst of our battles against the relentless attacks of the enemy. Prayer, along with the full armor of God, provides the necessary tools to persevere in the faith in the heart of battle.

SUMMARY

The believer is in a spiritual war against the forces of evil that are led by Satan. He has become the target of the evil one and therefore needs to prepare himself against the schemes of the devil. The weapons of Satan's hordes include persecution, deceptive lies, temptation, and disruption. In preparation, the believer needs to know the ways of his enemy in order to set up a good defense against his adversary. As God's soldier, the believer is commanded to put on the full armor of God to deflect the arrows of Satan. This armor includes six items. The belt of truth that is foundational to our defense and in which we stand firm against the diabolical schemes of Satan; the breastplate of righteousness, which protects us against ungodly behavior and disunity; the gospel of peace to drive out the fears we encounter in this life; the shield of faith to guard against unbelief; the helmet of salvation in which we cultivate the hope we have in Christ; the sword of the Spirit, the Word of God, to defend ourselves against the temptations of Satan. These pieces of armor along with the special privilege of coming to the Father in prayer provides us with the best defense against the relentless attacks of our enemy.

Chapter Nine

ESSENTIAL PRACTICES IN THE CHRISTIAN WALK

If I speak with the tongues of men and of angels, but do not have love, I have become a noisy gong or a clanging cymbal. If I have the gift of prophecy, and know all mysteries and all knowledge; and if I have all faith, so as to remove mountains, but do not have love, I am nothing. And if I give all my possessions to feed the poor, and if I surrender my body to be burned, but do not have love, it profits me nothing. (1 Corinthians 13:1-3)

LOVE

Love is the greatest expression of our Christian faith. It is the main ingredient that testifies to our calling in Christ. The Apostle Paul's words in the opening verse of the love chapter, above, are provoking. Without love we are just a *noisy gong or a clanging cymbal.* The intention of Paul is to show a parallel between a loud noise that comes to an immediate silence and a Christian walk without love. Loud noises get the attention of those who hear them but their sounds fade into immediate obscurity. The believer whose beliefs and practices are not governed with love will see his deeds die with time. His words of truth have a persuasive effect on people, but it is love in his actions that maintains the truth in the minds and hearts of his hearers.

It is difficult for a non-believer to capture the essence of God's love in its fundamental nature. The depths of His love are beyond their comprehension; however, this is not true with the believer. God has revealed His love to us in the Son and by the Holy Spirit. Jesus gave the disciples a new commandment, to love one another as He had loved them.

> *A new commandment I give to you, that you love one another, even as I have loved you, that you also love one another. "By this all men will know that you are My disciples, if you have love for one another."* (John 13:34-35)

The reason we can love in this manner is because our saving faith in Christ has provided us with access to the fullness of God's grace and love. The Holy Spirit that indwells all believers has illuminated the true character of love in our hearts. We, as believers, have personally experienced the love of Christ; therefore, we understand the depths of God's love toward all mankind. Our obligation to this insight and knowledge of love is to live a Spirit-filled life, and allow God's love to pour out of us in our actions toward others. The effects of our love on someone's life are profound and life changing to those who receive it.

A deception that we as individuals in the church have to guard against is a shallow understanding of God's love. There is an enormous difference between one who knows what God's Word says about love and one who practices it in his everyday life. Many of us believe we are one big love machine because we are familiar with all the Scriptures on love. We have a tendency to substitute the knowledge of love in Scripture in place of the practice of love toward others. It is good to grow in the knowledge of love as long as our hearts are continuing to grow in the love of Jesus Christ. Each one of us needs to examine our hearts daily to see if we are truly walking in God's love as revealed to us in the Scriptures.

The Essence of Love

Biblical love in its essence is not an emotional feeling, but an action that is directed at the well-being of others. It has at its core the characteristics of being unconditional and self-sacrificing toward the one that is loved. The unconditional nature of love works independently of another person's actions. The person who is truly loving someone biblically is not returning a favor or being kind to someone due to their previous actions, but treats them in a loving way without any ulterior motives. The self-sacrificing nature expresses the cost of love. It puts another person's concerns ahead of his own desires in order to meet the needs of others. The greatest expression of biblical love was at the cross when Christ died for our sins. He died for man, who was steeped in sin, as He sacrificed His own life for the sake of others. There was nothing in man that provoked Christ to this action; nevertheless, He went to the cross sacrificing His own life and demonstrating His love in all its fullness.

The Indispensable Nature of Love

The indispensable nature of love is revealed in Paul's words. He says that if you have not love, it profits you nothing. All of a believer's works add up to zero when he fails to apply love to his life. To illustrate this point, I would like to take you back to my childhood. When I was in first grade learning mathematics, multiplying numbers by zero was confusing to me. Perhaps this was because I learned addition and subtraction first. Addition was easy for me. One plus zero equals one. Two plus zero equals two. One hundred plus zero equals one hundred. There was no problem understanding that. All I had to do was bring the one number of value down and put it in the answer. Subtraction was no different. One minus zero equals one. Two minus zero equals two. One hundred minus zero equals one hundred. Once again there was no problem.

But when it came to multiplication it didn't come that easy. The teacher would ask me how much one times zero equaled. I would say one. She would say no and give me the answer of zero, and confusion would set in. Then she would ask me how much is two times zero. I would say two and she would say wrong and once again give me the answer of zero, leaving me in my perplexed state. Then she would ask me how much is one hundred times zero. I would think about it and conclude that it had to be at least fifty because one hundred is a huge number. After I stopped guessing, she explained to me that it was zero because no matter how big a number is, when it is multiplied by zero it equals zero. My problem was that I couldn't understand how an equation could equal zero when there was such a huge number in the equation. It had to at least equal something of a numeric value greater then zero. In time I was able to understand the concept of multiplication.

The application is this: the Apostle Paul is saying the same thing about a life without love. No matter how much we do for God, if it is not accompanied with love, it comes out to nothing and is unprofitable. Zero love times anything we do in the ministry will always come out to zero. This is because it is the love of God demonstrated in His child that moves the hearts of people to repentance and faith. Eloquent words and knowledge impact people's minds, but it is their hearts that need to be pierced with the truth. Our actions in love reinforce our words. Love becomes the means by which our words reach into people's hearts and make a lasting difference in their lives.

The Qualities of Love

In the Corinthian passage, Paul personifies love, revealing the qualities of its nature.

> *Love is patient, love is kind and is not jealous; love does not brag and is not arrogant, does not act unbecomingly; it does not seek its own, is not provoked, does not take into account a wrong suffered, does not rejoice in unrighteousness, but rejoices with the truth; bears all things, believes all things, hopes all things, endures all things. Love never fails.* (1 Corinthians 13:4-8a)

Love is patient and kind, always considerate and understanding toward others. It is never jealous, but rejoices with the blessings of others. It is never prideful, conceited, or rude, and always conducts itself in a proper manner toward all men. Love is a life that is Christ-centered and not self-centered. Love is always seeking the good of others and able to forgive their mistakes. Love is always faithful to the truth and rejoices in the truth, upholding righteousness in all truth. It always perseveres against the adversities of life, never losing faith or hope, enduring through the hardships and tribulations of circumstances. Love never fails and it is the foundation in which all other godly traits mature. It is persistent in its determination to love others. It can never be separated from the practice of faith in the believer's walk.

The greatest expression of our love for God is our love toward each other.

We love, because He first loved us. If someone says, "I love God," and hates his brother, he is a liar; for the one who does not love his brother whom he has seen, cannot love God whom he has not seen. And this commandment we have from Him, that the one who loves God should love his brother also. (1 John 4:19-21)

UNITY IN THE CHURCH

Love is the most essential practice in the Christian walk. The second most important matter is unity in the body of Christ. The oneness of God's people brings glory to the Father in heaven.

Now may the God who gives perseverance and encouragement grant you to be of the same mind with one another according to Christ Jesus, **so that with one accord you may with one voice glorify the God and Father** *of our Lord Jesus Christ. Therefore, accept one another, just as Christ also accepted us to the glory of God.* (Romans 15:5-7, emphasis added)

It is the obligation of every believer to maintain unity in the church. In Ephesians 4:1-6, the Apostle Paul tells us to preserve the unity in the body of Christ since God has provided everything necessary for us to live in harmony toward one another.

Therefore I, the prisoner of the Lord, implore you to walk in a manner worthy of the calling with which you have been called, with all humility and gentleness, with patience, showing tolerance for one another in love, being diligent **to preserve the unity** *of the Spirit in the bond of peace. There is one body and one Spirit, just as also you*

were called in one hope of your calling; one Lord, one
faith, one baptism, one God and Father of all who is over
all and through all and in all. (Ephesians 4:1-6, emphasis added)

One Father, one faith, one Savior, and one hope directs us all. The believer who is growing in genuine love protects and preserves the unity of the church in which the Holy Spirit has joined us together in one body. We all share a common purpose and goal in our service to God. This was the Apostle Paul's admonishment to the Philippians.

Therefore if there is any encouragement in Christ, if
there is any consolation of love, if there is any fellowship
of the Spirit, if any affection and compassion, make my
joy complete by being of the same mind, maintaining the
same love, united in spirit, intent on one purpose. Do
nothing from selfishness or empty conceit, but with
humility of mind regard one another as more important
than yourselves; do not merely look out for your own per-
sonal interests, but also for the interests of others.
(Philippians 2:1-4)

Since the Philippians all shared in the fellowship of God's love, they were to uphold the oneness of the body of Christ. They were to be united with the same mind, maintaining the same love with a common purpose to glorify the Father in heaven. They were to abandon all selfish and prideful conduct and walk in humility, regarding others more important than themselves. The result of this is a life that looks to the well-being of others and not one's self.

There is a strong correlation between the practice of love and maintaining the unity in the local church. It is impossible to keep the unity without individuals growing in the grace of love. Most problems or disruptions in the church are due to the immaturity of believers who fail to uphold the essence of love in their Christian lives. They are usually consumed in their self-centered ideas and ways with no consciousness or concern for the church as a whole. Selfish individual actions can sometimes have a devastating effect on the church. Without love, a believer becomes critical of the church, inviting other believers to join with him in his unbecoming attitude. It only takes a handful of people to begin the process of disrupting the unity in the church.

In the last chapter we discussed that one of Satan's means of destroying the church is by disrupting the fellowship of believers, especially among the leaders. Satan shops around a local church for one or two believers to implement his plan. He is persistent in this area and feeds on the immaturity of his selected targets to accomplish his purpose. It appears that this approach to his warfare has been very successful. Many people in local churches are blind to the ways of Satan, becoming his tools to do his damaging work. Everyone in their defense against Satan needs to be reminded of these two priorities, love and unity, in upholding the integrity of the local church.

Unity and Personal Convictions

Sometimes the believers initiate division in the body because of personal convictions. There have been judgmental attitudes between brothers because of the differences they share about certain issues in the church. We must understand that unity does not mean we all think the same way. There are a variety of opinions and convictions within the body of Christ. Some believers are able to partake of certain practices whereby another believer's convictions will not allow him. These issues, in which the believers share different viewpoints, are not specifically addressed in the Bible. They are left to the believers' conscience to determine how they will conduct themselves toward certain practices. If these practices are considered to be within the boundaries of God's Word, then the believers must be tolerant of one another's convictions. The different convictions that believers share should not disrupt the unity of the church or the common purpose.

The Apostle Paul in Romans 14 addresses this issue and gives us guidelines to follow when there are differences of opinions among believers. In verses 1-4, he asks the believers not to judge each other in the freedom of their practices.

> *Accept him whose faith is weak, without passing judgment on disputable matters. One man's faith allows him to eat everything, but another man, whose faith is weak, eats only vegetables. The man who eats everything must not look down on him who does not, and the man who does not eat everything must not condemn the man who does, for God has accepted him. Who are you to judge someone else's servant? To his own master he stands or falls. And he will stand, for the Lord is able to make him stand.* (Romans 14:1-4 NIV)

In order to understand these statements, we must recognize who and what is being addressed in the passage. Then we must define certain terms according to the context of the passage. Those who are being addressed are the *strong* and *weak* brothers (*accept him whose faith is weak*). The one who is asked to "accept him" is the strong brother, while the one "whose faith is weak" is the weak brother. We learn that the strong brother is defined as one who has freedom to partake of certain practices (disputable matters, verse 1) in which his conscience gives him liberty to participate in them. The weak brother is defined as one whose conscience bothers him about certain practices and therefore cannot partake of them. *Disputable matters* (verse 1) are issues or practices that are not sin in themselves (there is no specific law against them), but can become sin if practiced by an individual against his conscience.

In this context, the weak brother cannot partake of meat that was sold in the marketplace of the town. The reason was because the meat at one time might have been offered up to a pagan god and then brought to the marketplace in order to be sold. His conscience will not allow him to eat the meat since he feels that the ritual, performed prior to it being sold at the marketplace, contaminated the food. The strong brother is not bothered by that fact since he has reasoned that food cannot be affected by such a practice; therefore, his conscience allows him to partake of it without any reservations.

With that understanding, Paul makes five points in these verses pertaining to personal convictions. First, in verse 1, the strong brother is to accept the weak brother without trying to change his convictions.

Accept him whose faith is weak, without passing judgment on disputable matters.

The strong brother is not to look down on the weak brother or attempt to convince him to act contrary to his convictions. He is to accept his feelings on the matter even though he shares a different viewpoint. Second, in verse 2, Paul shows how believers can have different convictions when addressing the same matters or issues.

*One man's faith allows him to eat everything, but another
man, whose faith is weak, eats only vegetables.*

These are legitimate feelings by both the strong and the weak.
Third, in verse 3, the weak and the strong are not to judge each
other's convictions.

*The man who eats everything must not look down on him
who does not, and the man who does not eat everything
must not condemn the man who does, for God has
accepted him.*

In this verse, the strong brother is admonished to accept the
weak brother's convictions, and the weak brother is asked not to
condemn the freedom of the strong brother. The reason why is
because God has accepted them both according to their personal
convictions. In verse 4, Paul warns against this kind of judgment
toward each other.

*Who are you to judge someone else's servant? To his own
master he stands or falls. And he will stand, for the Lord is
able to make him stand.*

If God has accepted their legitimate convictions (strong and
weak), then how can one brother stand in judgment against
another brother's practices that are acceptable before God?

In verses 5-6, Paul continues with the emphasis put on the
heart and attitude of the believer in his practices.

*One man considers one day more sacred than another;
another man considers every day alike. Each one should be
fully convinced in his own mind. He who regards one day as*

special, does so to the Lord. He who eats meat, eats to the Lord, for he gives thanks to God; and he who abstains, does so to the Lord and gives thanks to God (Romans 14:5-6 NIV)

In verse 5, Paul shows the different convictions in relation to observing special days. One man considers one day more special than another day, another man considers all days alike. The point Paul is making is that every believer must be fully convinced in his heart and mind in what convictions he holds. The basis for a firm conviction is the motivation of the heart in the practice of these disputable matters. If a believer's practices are governed by a strong consciousness to please God in everything, his convictions are built on a strong foundation. If the believer is not inspired by this fact, the motives of his heart will be exposed at the judgment seat of God (see below). This is the point Paul is making in verses 7-12.

For none of us lives to himself alone and none of us dies to himself alone. If we live, we live to the Lord; and if we die, we die to the Lord. So, whether we live or die, we belong to the Lord. For this very reason, Christ died and returned to life so that he might be the Lord of both the dead and the living. You, then, why do you judge your brother? Or why do you look down on your brother? For we will all stand before God's judgment seat. It is written: "As surely as I live," says the Lord, "every knee will bow before me; every tongue will confess to God." So then, each of us will give an account of himself to God. (Romans 14:7-12 NIV)

This judgment of God will take place at the judgment seat of Christ in which the believer's works will be judged.

For we must all appear before the judgment seat of Christ,
so that each one may be recompensed for his deeds in the
body, according to what he has done, whether good or bad.
(2 Corinthians 5:10)

This judgment is not in relationship to sin, as the believer's sin was judged at the cross, but the judgment is according to the deeds done in the body of Christ. If the believer's works were produced by his love for God, his deeds will survive the judgment. If his deeds were self-gratifying or self-glorifying they will be burned up, but his salvation will not be affected. Paul alluded to this in 1 Corinthians.

...each man's work will become evident; for the day will
show it because it is to be revealed with fire, and the fire
itself will test the quality of each man's work. If any
man's work which he has built on it remains, he will
receive a reward. If any man's work is burned up, he will
suffer loss; but he himself will be saved, yet so as through
fire. (1 Corinthians 3:13-15)

Here is the point of the matter. If a believer is partaking of a certain practice because he is looking to satisfy himself with a disregard for the things of God, his heart and motive will be revealed at the judgment seat of Christ. At times one cannot know the heart of another person, but God does and so we should leave room for His judgment. *If a person has used his freedom in Christ to a fault* it will be revealed at the proper time. For the meantime, we should not pass judgment on another believer's convictions.

Therefore let us stop passing judgment on one another.
(Romans 14:13a NIV)

Verse 13 serves as a transition verse from the subject of judging each other to the principle of love in our personal convictions.

Therefore let us stop passing judgment on one another.
Instead, make up your mind not to put any stumbling
block or obstacle in your brother's way. (Romans 14:13 NIV)

Whereas verse 13a completes the thought of judgment towards one another in personal convictions, verse 13b introduces us to a new principle regarding this issue, the principle of love. The practices of our convictions are to be governed by the principle of love. Our love for our brothers supersedes any behavior we are free to partake of that may be offensive or stumbling to another brother. Paul addresses this in verses 14-21 of Romans 14:

As one who is in the Lord Jesus, I am fully convinced that
no food is unclean in itself. But if anyone regards some-
thing as unclean, then for him it is unclean. If your
brother is distressed because of what you eat, you are no
longer acting in love. Do not by your eating destroy your
brother for whom Christ died. Do not allow what you con-
sider good to be spoken of as evil. For the kingdom of God
is not a matter of eating and drinking, but of righteous-
ness, peace and joy in the Holy Spirit, because anyone who
serves Christ in this way is pleasing to God and approved
by men. Let us therefore make every effort to do what
leads to peace and to mutual edification. Do not destroy
the work of God for the sake of food. All food is clean, but
it is wrong for a man to eat anything that causes someone
else to stumble. It is better not to eat meat or drink wine
or to do anything else that will cause your brother to fall.
(NIV)

In verse 14, Paul is convinced that no food is unclean in itself; but if another believer cannot accept that in his conscience, then for him it is unclean. Paul knows that what he practices is lawful; but since his brother does not share the same convictions, his actions run the risk of stumbling him. That is, his brother might be enticed to partake of the same practice against his will, wounding his conscience in his worship of God. Therefore, in love, he refrains from partaking of something that is stumbling to another brother. The application is this, when the practice of our convictions becomes detrimental or stumbling to a brother, the principle of love needs to be engaged. This is pleasing to God (verse 18) and leads to peace and edification in the body of Christ (verse 19). Let us not lose sight of the bigger picture of God's plan for His church, love and unity, which go far beyond our own personal convictions.

Paul's concluding comments are words of wisdom to the strong and weak brother.

> *So whatever you believe about these things keep between yourself and God. Blessed is the man who does not condemn himself by what he approves. But the man who has doubts is condemned if he eats, because his eating is not from faith; and everything that does not come from faith is sin.* (Romans 14:22-23 NIV)

If the strong brother's faith allows him freedom to participate in something, he is to keep it between God and himself, in order not to stumble another brother, thereby bringing condemnation upon his actions. If the weak brother's conscience convicts him, then he must refrain from participating in certain practices. Sin is committed because he is no longer acting in faith, and is going against what his conscience is telling him.

Paul's application to all this is given in chapter 15.

*We who are strong ought to bear with the failings of the
weak and not to please ourselves. Each of us should please
his neighbor for his good, to build him up. For even Christ
did not please himself but, as it is written: "The insults of
those who insult you have fallen on me." For everything
that was written in the past was written to teach us, so
that through endurance and the encouragement of the
Scriptures we might have hope. May the God who gives
endurance and encouragement give you a spirit of unity
among yourselves as you follow Christ Jesus, so that with
one heart and mouth you may glorify the God and Father
of our Lord Jesus Christ. Accept one another, then, just as
Christ accepted you, in order to bring praise to God.*
(Romans 15:1-7 NIV)

When every believer is pursuing love and doing everything in
his power to preserve the unity of the church, the results will be
profound. The church will be strengthened, growing in the grace
and knowledge of Jesus Christ. The believers will walk in harmony toward one another, and the church will protect itself
against the schemes of Satan with a strong defense that cannot be
penetrated. The most excellent result is that the Father in heaven
will be glorified in our oneness and love (cf. Romans 15:6-7).

THE ACT OF GIVING

The third practice essential to the church saint is the obligation
of every believer to give financially to maintain the needs of the
church. We learn in the book of Acts that the church is self-sup-
porting. The church should not have to depend on the government

or resources outside the body of Christ in order to function financially. This third item is sometimes difficult to present from the pulpit since many today in the congregation are defensive when it comes to money. There have been many charlatans in the past who have manipulated the church as a whole. These swindlers should not deter the church from this vital practice, which is necessary for the welfare of the church. The issue of giving is a biblical principle and the obligation and responsibility of every believer in his service to God.

Pivotal Principles on Giving

The foundational passages to the church on giving are found in 2 Corinthians 8 and 9. Studying these chapters reveals many lessons concerning this essential practice. To begin with, poverty is not an excuse for not giving.

Now, brethren, we wish to make known to you the grace of God which has been given in the churches of Macedonia, that in a great ordeal of affliction their abundance of joy and their **deep poverty** *overflowed in the wealth of their liberality.* (2 Corinthians 8:1-2, emphasis added)

Paul commends these believers in Macedonia for their generosity in giving abundantly, despite their deep poverty. Their financial situation did not deter them from the special privilege of giving to the needs of others. The passage goes on to say that they gave "of their own accord" that is, a personal desire, wanting to give.

For I testify that according to their ability, and beyond their ability, they gave of their own accord, begging us with much urging for the favor of participation in the support of the saints. (2 Corinthians 8:3-4)

The second lesson we learn from these verses is that the believer should always give from his heart and not under compulsion. Giving out of guilt is not an acceptable offering before God. The believers above not only gave generously, but also were delighted to share in this act of giving. God loves a cheerful giver (cf. 2 Corinthians 9:7), therefore, the believer's giving should be prompted by this proper attitude. When this is true, his giving is an acceptable offering before God.

Third, giving comes freely when we first give ourselves to the service of the Lord.

> *...and this, not as we had expected, but they first gave themselves to the Lord and to us by the will of God.*
> (2 Corinthians 8:5)

When a believer is committed to the work of God, his priority in giving will be for the welfare of God's kingdom on earth. He will look for ways in which he can serve the church by sharing with individuals or ministries that are in financial need.

Fourth, Paul admonishes the believers to abound in this practice.

> *But just as you abound in everything, in faith and utterance and knowledge and in all earnestness and in the love we inspired in you, see that you abound in this gracious work also.* (2 Corinthians 8:7)

The believer's obligation of giving should increase in this special privilege as he matures in the faith. He should abound in giving, looking for ways to invest more of his income for the kingdom of God. Although some teach that a 10 percent tithe is the obligation of every believer, the New Testament nowhere commands this of the church saint. Tithing is an Old Testament concept and is never used in conjunction with the church. It is mentioned in the Gospels in relation to the Pharisees and Jewish leaders (cf. Matthew 23:23; Luke 11:42) who were still under the Law. With the coming of Christ the Law came to an end (cf. Romans 10:4). This is not to suggest that the New Testament believer's obligation to give came to an end with the Law, but his giving is governed by a new principle, as laid out in this pivotal passage. *Give under grace and excel in this special privilege.* We should give according to the proportion of our income (cf. 1 Corinthians 16:1-2) with the intention of giving more as we grow in our Christian faith. Some have suggested 10 percent as a rule of thumb by using the examples of Abraham and Jacob (Genesis 14:20; 28:22). This may be a good example to follow but don't stop at 10 percent, continue to abound in this privilege of giving to God. This is possible as we maintain our priorities in order to give freely to the work of God.

The fifth lesson is that our giving is an expression of our love for God.

I am not speaking this as a command, but as proving through the earnestness of others the sincerity of your love also. (2 Corinthians 8:8)

Sixth, the believer should look to Jesus Christ in this sacrifice of giving. Christ was the ultimate example as He gave everything of Himself for the sake of others.

For you know the grace of our Lord Jesus Christ, that though He was rich, yet for your sake He became poor, so that you through His poverty might become rich. (2 Corinthians 8:9)

The seventh lesson is that giving brings equality to the church in material needs.

> *For this is not for the ease of others and for your affliction, but by way of equality—at this present time your abundance being a supply for their need, so that their abundance also may become a supply for your need, that there may be equality; as it is written, "HE WHO gathered MUCH DID NOT HAVE TOO MUCH, AND HE WHO gathered LITTLE HAD NO LACK."* (2 Corinthians 8:13-15)

When the church as a whole is faithful to giving, then the financial needs of the faithful poor will be met. No one will be in need and every member can devote himself to the work of God.

SUMMARY

There are three essential practices in the church that every member must uphold in order to maintain the integrity and character of the local church. The first is love, which is the main ingredient that solidifies the body. Love is the foundational trait in which the body grows in the attributes of Christ. The second practice is the obligation of every member to protect and maintain the unity of the church. When each believer is diligent in safeguarding and preserving the unity, the church functions harmoniously, bringing glory to the Father. The third practice is giving to the needs of the church. When each member gives generously, no faithful member will be in need. The church can function without the burden of financial problems and continue to promote the truth of the gospel message worldwide.

Chapter Ten

THE PRACTICE OF RIGHTEOUSNESS

Let love be without hypocrisy. Abhor what is evil; cling to what is good. Be devoted to one another in brotherly love; give preference to one another in honor; not lagging behind in diligence, fervent in spirit, serving the Lord; rejoicing in hope, persevering in tribulation, devoted to prayer, contributing to the needs of the saints, practicing hospitality. Bless those who persecute you; bless and do not curse. Rejoice with those who rejoice, and weep with those who weep. Be of the same mind toward one another; do not be haughty in mind, but associate with the lowly. Do not be wise in your own estimation. Never pay back evil for evil to anyone. Respect what is right in the sight of all men. If possible, so far as it depends on you, be at peace with all men. Never take your own revenge, beloved, but leave room for the wrath of God, for it is written, "Vengeance is Mine, I will repay," says the Lord. "But if your enemy is hungry, feed him, and if he is thirsty, give him a drink; for in so doing you will heap burning coals on His head." Do not be overcome by evil, but overcome evil with good.

(Romans 12:9-21)

THE VARIOUS EXPRESSIONS OF RIGHTEOUSNESS

The above passage reveals many practices pertaining to Christian conduct. This pivotal passage on righteousness touches on almost every area of the Christian walk. It serves as a compact manual on how the believer is to express his righteousness in Christ, in his daily worship of God. We would do well to follow in the footsteps of these practices that direct us in our everyday life.

A Genuine Love

Love is the first issue addressed. As previously mentioned in chapter 9, love is the foundation for all other godly traits to grow in our lives. Paul tells the believers that their love must be without hypocrisy; that is, a love that is not shallow or without substance, but is genuine and operates in all truth. Our love should be real and unconditional and reflect the character of Jesus Christ in His love for us. The practice of love gives strength and weight to the truth we proclaim, and is a powerful means of gaining a hearing for the gospel message. People who are the recipients of our love are more inclined to hear our testimony of salvation and the truth of Jesus Christ.

Abhor What Is Evil

The believer is to "*abhor what is evil.*" To *abhor* is to express a hatred for something by separating oneself from it. *Evil* in this text means something that opposes the good. We are to express our hatred for evil by separating ourselves from the practices and beliefs of the world which oppose the clear teaching of God's Word. Righteousness, in this context, is defined by separation from ungodliness. We are not to partake of anything that hinders our walk or our witness to the gospel message. Refraining from this conduct is a statement of our loyalty to the truth of Jesus Christ.

Cling to What Is Good

The believer is to "cling to what is good." The word *cling* carries the meaning of gluing oneself to something. We as God's people are to unite ourselves completely with Christ in righteousness and follow Him wherever He guides us. The conduct that reveals the goodness and purity of God is the path every Christian should walk.

Devoted to One Another

In the family of God, we are to be affectionate to one another with brotherly love. Our relationship to brothers and sisters in the Lord is to be as strong as our family ties. Our brothers and sisters, who are our partners in proclaiming the gospel message, should be precious and dear to us since they partake of the common purpose of glorifying the Father. Sharing our lives with one another results in an intimate bond of friendship.

Give Preference to One Another in Honor

We are to "give preference to one another in honor" (verse 10), regarding others as more important than ourselves. In our humility, there should be a transformation in which we become people-centered, abandoning our self-centered ways. We should become consumed in the needs of others and less concerned with our personal needs and desires. Jesus Christ will meet our personal needs as our Lord and Savior.

The Pace and Intensity of the Christian Walk

The pace and intensity of our walk with God is revealed in verse 11. We are to be attentive to spiritual matters, *not lagging behind in diligence, fervent in spirit, serving the Lord.* To put it in other terms, we should be on fire for God at all times. Anything less than this stifles us from walking in the fullness of our faith.

There is only one speed in which the believer operates properly in his service to God: full speed ahead.

In order to maintain this pace in our walk, verse 12 mentions three things. First, we should always rejoice in the hope of God's promises. Biblical hope is not like the hope the world has in which there remains an uncertainty of tomorrow, but the hope of the believer is the absolute assurance of tomorrow. This is why the Apostle Peter called it a living hope, since it produces a joy in our present reality knowing that God's promises will come to pass.

> *Blessed be the God and Father of our Lord Jesus Christ,*
> *who according to His great mercy has caused us to be born*
> *again* **to a living hope** *through the resurrection of Jesus*
> *Christ from the dead, to obtain an inheritance which is*
> *imperishable and undefiled and will not fade away,*
> *reserved in heaven for you, who are protected by the power*
> *of God through faith for a salvation ready to be revealed*
> *in the last time.* (1 Peter 1:3-5, emphasis added)

Our joy in life should emanate from the blessed hope that we all share in Jesus Christ. This alone should be enough for us to be joyful always, unhindered by the state of affairs surrounding us. The Bible teaches that the joy of our salvation can never be dampened by the circumstances of life. There should always be present an inexpressible joy that is simmering in our innermost being, knowing that God will uphold all His promises to us.

Second, we should be patient in our hardships and tribulations, persevering through our trials in a God-honoring way. The disciples were warned in the gospel account of troubles in this world, but the peace of God would sustain them through the adversity of these times.

These things I have spoken to you, so that in Me you may have peace. In the world you have tribulation, but take courage; I have overcome the world. (John 16:33)

Our understanding of trials as part of God's plan protects us from stalling in our Christian walk. Instead of letting trials discourage us, we look at them as opportunities to testify to the faith that we profess. Our courage and ability to maintain our poise in the midst of tribulations is a strong witness to those who oppose the gospel.

Third, we are to remain devoted to prayer in our daily life. Devotion means to give constant attention to the special privilege of approaching God in prayer. We are to be persistent in our prayer life, especially when our request is worthy and according to the will of God. Prayer is what helps us maintain our fellowship with God and keep our focus on the things that are true and eternal in the midst of adversities. All three items—rejoicing in hope, patience in tribulations, and our dedication to prayer—help us maintain our pace and intensity in our Christian walk.

Providing for One Another

In verse 13, we are further instructed on proper practices in the fellowship of believers. Our obligation is to meet the material needs of others. Our fellowship should be aware of any financial struggles or material issues that burden faithful brothers. When a brother in Christ has upheld his obligation to God and the gospel, then the church should provide any necessary help to that faithful saint. We are also to practice and seek opportunities in showing hospitality when it is in our power to act. When Paul wrote this letter it was important that the church supported itinerant preachers who traveled miles on foot to preach the gospel. They needed a place to rest and find comfort after their long trek across the land. Although travel is definitely more suitable today for the gospel, there are many Christians who are relocating their lives and ministries who would welcome the hospitality of fellow saints. To find kindness among the believers is a precious thing in offsetting the stress of moving. There are also many missionaries who are visiting on furlough who could use a home-cooked meal and an atmosphere of kindness in overcoming their weariness from the mission field.

Enduring Persecution

In verse 14, the believer is instructed on how to handle persecution: *Bless those who persecute you; bless and do not curse.* When we are under fire, our flesh can dictate how we respond. Our first inclination is to retaliate, but God wants us to react in the same manner as Christ. We are to constantly return kindness and love to those who mistreat us. A good passage to follow in confronting any adversity of this nature is Paul's word of encouragement to Timothy:

> *The Lord's bond-servant must not be quarrelsome, but be kind to all, able to teach, patient when wronged, with gentleness correcting those who are in opposition, if perhaps God may grant them repentance leading to the knowledge of the truth, and they may come to their senses and escape from the snare of the devil, having been held captive by him to do his will.* (2 Timothy 2:24-26)

In our battle against hatred and evil, we must consider the role of Satan in blinding people to the truth. Doing so helps us to be patient and considerate with those who are lost. An act of kindness and understanding toward hatred is something that most people respond to in a favorable way. Even the most hard-core criminal can have a change of heart toward those who return kindness for his evil ways. Why is this so important? The godly reaction of kindness in the midst of adversity is what chips away at the hardness of a person's heart. God is concerned about the souls of people whose salvation is at stake. In persecution, the believer needs to see the bigger picture of God's program that is going on in heaven. The inconvenience of persecution is petty compared to the potential opportunity to win someone to the faith by reacting in the proper way. It is of utmost importance that in times of persecution we react like Christ, seeing our circumstances through the eyes of God.

Empathy in our Fellowship

In verse 15, we are called to rejoice with those who rejoice, and weep with those who weep. To rejoice with others is to share in their joy before God. I believe one of the greatest factors in binding us together in fellowship is sharing in each other's joy in our service to God. There is something wonderful in our friendships when we partake of each other's blessings in the Lord. It builds an intimate relationship of oneness as co-workers in our service to God. Whether we are the one who is being blessed or not, the important thing is that we can take pleasure together in each other's joy.

The opposite of rejoicing with those who rejoice is jealousy. The base of operation for jealousy is a self-centered attitude. The believer who reacts with jealousy to someone else's blessings is giving in to his self-centered ways, and robbing himself of his own joy. Instead of sharing in the joy of others, he responds selfishly. Jealousy is a killer that paralyzes the whole body from experiencing the joy and peace of the Holy Spirit. The book of Proverbs said it best:

Wrath is fierce and anger is a flood, But who can stand before jealousy? (Proverbs 27:4)

Believers are not only called to share their joy, but also to have empathy for each other when a brother or sister is in distress. We are to be sensitive, identifying with each other's troubles, and feeling some degree of pain for their circumstances. There is comfort for hurting people when others share the burden with them. Only by growing in the love of Christ can we develop a genuine concern in which we are considerate and sensitive to those who have come across hard times. Apart from this love, our empathy for others might be superficial and shallow, identifying with someone in word only and not with our heart.

Walk in Harmony

In verse 16 the saints are instructed to have the same mind toward one another. If we as people are to function in the one-ness of the Holy Spirit, then we need to have a common goal and purpose in our thinking. This was Paul's admonition to the Philippians:

If therefore there is any encouragement in Christ, if there is any consolation of love, if there is any fellowship of the Spirit, if any affection and compassion, make my joy complete by being of the same mind, maintaining the same love, united in spirit, intent on one purpose.
(Philippians 2:1-2)

By being of the same mind, we will pursue a course of action in which we each look to glorify the Father with the God-given abilities He has given us. Our actions will uphold the highest love for one another and the unity of the Holy Spirit. This same mind will direct us to share the task of bringing glory to the name of Jesus Christ.

We are not to set our minds on high things, but to associate with the humble (verse 16). Every believer should have the same love and enthusiasm toward all people, no matter what their social status may be. As believers we sometimes bring in our prejudices, relating differently to certain people in the church. Members are more inclined to gravitate to people of high standing, who may be leaders of the church or people of importance in their congregations. Many times those who need our attention in low positions are neglected because of the failure of the saint to uphold this practice. It is the hurting and those in humble positions that demand our encouragement and consideration. In James' letter to the believers he asked them to guard against this attitude in the church:

> *Dear brothers, how can you claim that you belong to the*
> *Lord Jesus Christ, the Lord of glory, if you show favoritism*
> *to rich people and look down on poor people? If a man*
> *comes into your church dressed in expensive clothes and*
> *with valuable gold rings on his fingers, and at the same*
> *moment another man comes in who is poor and dressed in*
> *threadbare clothes, and you make a lot of fuss over the rich*
> *man and give him the best seat in the house and say to the*
> *poor man, "You can stand over there if you like or else sit*
> *on the floor"—well, judging a man by his wealth shows*
> *that you are guided by wrong motives. Listen to me, dear*
> *brothers: God has chosen poor people to be rich in faith,*
> *and the Kingdom of Heaven is theirs, for that is the gift*
> *God has promised to all those who love him. And yet, of*
> *the two strangers, you have despised the poor man. Don't*
> *you realize that it is usually the rich men who pick on you*

and drag you into court? And all too often they are the ones who laugh at Jesus Christ, whose noble name you bear. Yes indeed, it is good when you truly obey our Lord's command, "You must love and help your neighbors just as much as you love and take care of yourself." But you are breaking this law of our Lord's when you favor the rich and fawn over them; it is sin. (James 2:1-9 TLB)

It is a sad picture of God's impartial love to man when a believer violates this command in the church setting. Believers need to look at all people through the eyes and heart of Jesus Christ. To Christ, an underprivileged person is as precious as anyone else in the congregation. The secular world has written off many people because of their unfortunate circumstances. God forgive us if we allow that kind of standard to govern our hearts in the treatment of others. Love the rich man and love the most popular man, but most of all love those in the church who have been deprived of encouragement and love by this world.

The last item in verse 16 has to do with the way we think, "Do not be wise in our own estimation." In order for this to be true, the believer must walk in humility. Humility helps us to see ourselves in light of God's holiness. This protects us against our prideful ways (thinking too much of ourselves) that blind us from divine understanding. The issue of pride is something that affects all believers. The man who is wise in his own eyes forfeits the grace that God provides in every given situation.

"God is opposed to the proud but gives grace to the humble." (James 4:6)

Trusting God and acknowledging Him in all our ways will protect the believers against a prideful attitude.

Trust in the LORD with all your heart And do not lean on your own understanding. In all your ways acknowledge Him, And He will make your paths straight. Do not be wise in your own eyes; Fear the LORD and turn away from evil. (Proverbs 3:5-7)

Never Pay Back Evil for Evil

In verse 17, the believer is instructed never to repay "evil for evil." Retaliation is never an option for the believer. In moments when we have been wronged, it is of utmost importance that the Holy Spirit guides us through those times. When the Spirit leads us, we will react with the grace and love of God and forsake our fleshly inclinations. Entrusting ourselves to the Father against adversity and hatred is the option that God wants us to choose. Jesus Christ left us a great example, which we would do well to follow. Peter reminded the believers of this godly example in his first epistle.

To this you were called, because Christ suffered for you, leaving you an example, that you should follow in his steps. "He committed no sin, and no deceit was found in his mouth." When they hurled their insults at him, he did not retaliate; when he suffered, he made no threats. Instead, he entrusted himself to him who judges justly. He himself bore our sins in his body on the tree, so that we might die to sins and live for righteousness; by his wounds you have been healed. For you were like sheep going astray, but now you have returned to the Shepherd and Overseer of your souls. (1 Peter 2:21-25 NIV)

Respect What Is Right in the Sight of All Men

The second issue in verse 17 is to "respect what is right in the sight of all men." God is asking us to conduct ourselves before man in a manner worthy of the gospel (cf. Philippians 1:27). Our lives should reflect the holiness, grace, and love of God in our conduct toward everyone. The purpose behind this is to enhance the message we proclaim and gain a hearing in the hearts of those who are listening. We are to submit ourselves to the conscience of all men *without compromising the truth*, in order to provide an opportunity for the preaching of the gospel message. The Apostle Paul gives us a personal testimony in 1 Corinthians chapter 9, for upholding this truth. Paul began the chapter with the rights he had as an apostle (1 Corinthians 9:1-12), but he chose not to exercise those rights in order not to hinder the gospel message (1 Corinthians 9:13,15). He was entitled to support from the church, but he chose not to apply that right in order to silence the critics who accused him of preaching the gospel for monetary gain (1 Corinthians 9:15-18). He forsook his own rights as an apostle, in order to gain the confidence of his hearers. He knew that the integrity of his life would win their approval, thereby preventing the gospel message from being hindered.

Paul goes on to show the principle that should govern our lives in our interaction with those outside the church.

> *Though I am free and belong to no man, I make myself a slave to everyone, to win as many as possible. To the Jews I became like a Jew, to win the Jews. To those under the law I became like one under the law (though I myself am not under the law), so as to win those under the law. To those not having the law I became like one not having the law (though I am not free from God's law but am under Christ's law), so as to win those not having the law. To the weak I became weak, to win the weak. I have become all things to all men so that by all possible means I might save some.* **I do all this for the sake of the gospel,** *that I may share in its blessings.* (1 Corinthians 9:19-23, emphasis added NIV)

Paul went to great lengths to do what was right in the sight of all men. He submitted himself to the convictions of others without compromising his own convictions before God. Every believer should share Paul's convictions in being a witness to the truth of God's Word. We cannot afford to lose sight of God's plan for man, salvation in Jesus Christ. Therefore, we must be willing at times to give up the rights that our flesh demands, in the hope of winning the lost to Jesus Christ.

Seek Peace with All Men

In verse 18, we are admonished to seek peace with all men. *(If possible, so far as it depends on you, be at peace with all men.)*. The verse allows for the possibility of some who are irreconcilable in promoting peace. Nonetheless, we are called to use our God-given wisdom and grace to avoid confrontation. In verse 19, we are not to avenge ourselves against the injustice directed at us, but to leave judgment for God. In this way, the opportunity is given for us to minister to our enemies. *(But if your enemy is hungry, feed him, and if he is thirsty, give him a drink, verse 20.)* The Father in heaven will make all things right at the proper time. The expression in verse 20, to *"heap burning coals on his head,"* could be referring to the burning pain of shame and remorse that a man feels when his hostility is repaid by love. This is further supported in verse 21 in which the final admonition of the passage tells us not to be *"overcome by evil, but overcome evil with good."* We are not to give into the temptation of retaliation, but are to continue to operate in God's love toward our adversaries.

CONCLUSION

In leaving this chapter it is essential that the believers take heed to James' admonishment in his epistle.

*Therefore, putting aside all filthiness and all that remains
of wickedness, in humility receive the word implanted,
which is able to save your souls.* **But prove yourselves
doers of the word, and not merely hearers** *who delude
themselves. For if anyone is a hearer of the word and not a
doer, he is like a man who looks at his natural face in a
mirror; for once he has looked at himself and gone away,
he has immediately forgotten what kind of person he was.*
(James 1:21-24, emphasis added)

The believer is to guard against an empty righteousness.
Knowing what the Word of God says and not acting upon it is a
sad commentary for God's ambassador. The believer is to constantly remind himself to put into practice the things he knows
to be true in God's Word. If he fails in this area, his Christian life
is just a shadow with no depth to his righteousness. Let us be
doers of God's Word, not just hearers.

*Be imitators of God, therefore, as dearly loved children
and live a life of love, just as Christ loved us and gave
himself up for us as a fragrant offering and sacrifice to
God.* (Ephesians 5:1-2 NIV)

Chapter Eleven

THE CHARACTER OF FAITH

Now faith is being sure of what we hope for and certain of what we do not see. This is what the ancients were commended for.
(Hebrews 11:1-2 NIV)

This description of faith, above, characterized the great saints of the Old Testament. They believed God; therefore, God commended them. They never wavered in the hope of God's promises and were certain of the things that were still to come. These were men and women who blazed a trail for the advancement of God's kingdom on earth. They persevered through the worst of times and never compromised what they knew to be right before God.

Chapter 11 of the book of Hebrews has much to say about the issue of faith. It has been called at times, the *hall of faith*, because it lists the names of many whose lives were governed by genuine faith in God Almighty. It records the great men and women of history, who left their mark upon this world by trusting in God.

THE VARIOUS EXAMPLES OF FAITH

The various displays of faith in the Old Testament saints are demonstrated throughout the verses of Hebrews 11. In addressing them we will see the many dimensions of faith that characterized their lives. In so doing, we will be encouraged to follow these examples of faith in our own lives.

The Belief of Faith

In verse 3, faith is the means by which we accept the testimony of Scripture.

> *By faith we understand that the worlds were prepared by the word of God, so that what is seen was not made out of things which are visible.* (Hebrews 11:3)

This is the belief of faith in which the believer is fully convinced in his heart that God's Word can be trusted. Although none of us were present during the creation of the world, the believers trust the Genesis record because God has revealed it in His Word. This is not to suggest a brainless faith that is based upon a hunch or a good feeling, but a faith with conviction that is absolutely certain beyond a shadow of a doubt. This conviction in our heart is brought about by God's faithfulness to everything He has said. Those of us who have tasted the goodness of God's Word through faith, and have witnessed its flawlessness in our lives, attest to the integrity of the Scriptures. The believer who trusts in God will accept the authenticity of God's Word from Genesis to Revelation. As God's people we cannot afford to waver in our beliefs. If God has said it, we can believe it. The belief of faith takes to heart the truth of God's Word.

The Righteousness of Faith

In verse 4, a contrast in conduct between Cain and Abel is revealed.

> *By faith Abel offered to God a better sacrifice than Cain,*
> *through which he obtained the testimony that he was*
> *righteous, God testifying about his gifts, and through faith,*
> *though he is dead, he still speaks.* (Hebrews 11:4)

Abel offered God a better sacrifice than Cain. Abel's sacrifice illustrates the *righteousness of faith*. The heart of Abel is what prompted him to bring a better sacrifice, which was acceptable to God. His faith was verified by his righteous act, done in obedience to the revealed will of God. A pure and righteous heart that is pleasing to the Lord will produce the fruit of righteousness. Apart from the right heart, one is clinging to a nominal faith. This was James' intention in his epistle—to protect against an empty faith that had no evidence to substantiate it.

> *What good is it, my brothers, if a man claims to have*
> *faith but has no deeds? Can such faith save him? Suppose*
> *a brother or sister is without clothes and daily food. If*
> *one of you says to him, "Go, I wish you well; keep warm*
> *and well fed," but does nothing about his physical needs,*
> *what good is it? In the same way, faith by itself, if it is*
> *not accompanied by action, is dead. But someone will*
> *say, "You have faith; I have deeds." Show me your faith*
> *without deeds, and I will show you my faith by what I*
> *do. You believe that there is one God. Good! Even the*
> *demons believe that—and shudder. You foolish man, do*
> *you want evidence that faith without deeds is useless?*
> *Was not our ancestor Abraham considered righteous for*

what he did when he offered his son Isaac on the altar?
You see that his faith and his actions were working
together, and his faith was made complete by what he
did. And the scripture was fulfilled that says, "Abraham
believed God, and it was credited to him as righteous-
ness," and he was called God's friend. You see that a per-
son is justified by what he does and not by faith alone. In
the same way, was not even Rahab the prostitute consid-
ered righteous for what she did when she gave lodging to
the spies and sent them off in a different direction? As the
body without the spirit is dead, so faith without deeds is
dead. (James 2:14-26 NIV)

Biblical faith is always accompanied with actions or righteous deeds. Empty faith is a profession of belief in God that
goes no further than the words one speaks. It is belief without
a trust in God. As James mentioned in this passage, even the
demons believe in one God, but one is hard pressed to convince us that demons are in heaven for their faith. In verse 24,
James is not saying that works are necessary for salvation, but
that works authenticate a genuine faith in God. There is no way
someone can say they believe in God and not turn from their
sin or even produce the smallest amount of fruit in their lives.
That would be totally inconsistent with biblical faith as it is
revealed in the Bible.

We are saved by faith alone, but faith reveals itself by trusting in the atoning work of Christ at the cross for our sins with
a total commitment in obedience to the teaching of His Word.
Our faith in God has a goal, which is to produce the fruit of
righteousness as witnesses who testify to the truth of God's
Word. Let our belief in God be characterized by the righteousness of faith.

The Value of Faith

In verse 5, the *precious value of faith* before God is revealed in the life of Enoch.

> *By faith Enoch was taken up so that he would not see death; AND HE WAS NOT FOUND BECAUSE GOD TOOK HIM UP; for he obtained the witness that before his being taken up he was pleasing to God.* (Hebrews 11:5)

The only thing we know about Enoch's life is that his ways were always pleasing to God. What a testimony of one man's life before God. From start to finish he lived to please the Father, knowing what was precious before God in heaven. In a world where man's value system is defined by money, fame, and material things, Enoch pursued a life of faith that was more valuable than all the treasures of this world. Peter, in his epistle spoke of the priceless value of one's faith before God.

> *These trials are only to test your faith, to see whether or not it is strong and pure. It is being tested as fire tests gold and purifies it*—**and your faith is far more precious to God than mere gold;** *so if your faith remains strong after being tried in the test tube of fiery trials, it will bring you much praise and glory and honor on the day of his return.*
> (1 Peter 1:7, emphasis added TLB)

In this context, Peter is directing the believers to the final product of a tested faith. He encourages the believers to persevere through the hardships of life and not to be discouraged. Their trials were the means God used to purify and strengthen their faith. James also encouraged the believers in this manner.

Consider it all joy, my brethren, when you encounter various trials, knowing that the testing of your faith produces endurance. And let endurance have its perfect result, so that you may be perfect and complete, lacking in nothing.
(James 1:2-4)

The believer who understands the value of genuine faith rejoices at the thought of what his trials are doing in his personal life. These trials fade in comparison to the spiritual riches that are produced in us who persevere through them in faith. The final product of a tested faith is a trust in God that is unmovable. A faith-filled life is precious in the eyes of God.

The Indispensable Nature of Faith

In verse 6, the indispensable nature of faith is attested to in the Christian walk.

And without faith it is impossible to please Him, for he who comes to God must believe that He is and that He is a rewarder of those who seek Him. (Hebrews 11:6)

Whereas Enoch's life was pleasing to the Lord, the Jewish believers referred to in this letter were displeasing God by returning to the Law. They were substituting the Jewish Law in the practice of their faith. They were making the same mistake that many people in the church are making today, *substituting some other means beside faith for pleasing God.*

Many today in the church have moved away from this basic principle, *"the righteous shall live by faith,"* without realizing it. They began their Christian lives by putting their faith in Christ, but in time they failed to live by faith on a daily basis for their spiritual and physical needs. They profess to have faith, but their actions indicate otherwise, failing to stand on the Word of God alone. In many cases, their faith is defined by mimicking Christian practices in the church without personally trusting in God in their daily lives. The believer today needs to guard against this false expression of faith, by trusting in the Word of God alone and applying it whenever it is applicable. A healthy faith in God is always defined by acting upon what we know to be true. We must participate in the church, but not allow that to become the criteria for measuring our faith, especially if we are failing to trust in God in the privacy of our own lives.

The Apostle Paul, knowing the vital role of faith, prayed for the saints that Christ might dwell in their hearts through faith.

> *For this reason I bow my knees before the Father, from whom every family in heaven and on earth derives its name, that He would grant you, according to the riches of His glory, to be strengthened with power through His Spirit in the inner man,* **so that Christ may dwell in your hearts through faith;** *and that you, being rooted and grounded in love, may be able to comprehend with all the saints what is the breadth and length and height and depth, and to know the love of Christ which surpasses knowledge, that you may be filled up to all the fullness of God.* (Ephesians 3:14-19, emphasis added)

Placing our trust in God on a continuous basis is what strengthens us, providing us with the necessary grace in our Christian walk. When we come to God in this manner, we will fully understand the depths of God's love and grow in the full knowledge of Jesus Christ. The indispensable nature of faith in the Christian walk cannot be overestimated.

The Perseverance of Faith

The perseverance of faith is demonstrated in the life of Noah in verse 7.

> *By faith Noah, being warned by God about things not yet seen, in reverence prepared an ark for the salvation of his household, by which he condemned the world, and became an heir of the righteousness which is according to faith.*
> (Hebrews 11:7)

Noah was instructed by God to build an ark that would take 120 years to build (cf. Genesis 6:3). Although we are not given the details of this time, Noah probably came under much ridicule. It had never before rained, and God's instructions to build a boat against the possibility of a flood seemed impossible. Noah never wavered in his commitment to God. He persevered through all the ridicule and unbelief that surrounded his faith-filled life. The faith of Noah portrays a man who received direction from God and continued in that path until the goal was reached. In the same way, the believer today needs to persevere through the persecution and unbelief that permeates society. He is to continue in his faith, despite opposition, until he is taken home to be with the Lord in heaven.

The Obedience of Faith

The obedience of faith is emphasized in the life of Abraham.

> *By faith Abraham, when he was called, obeyed by going out to a place which he was to receive for an inheritance; and he went out, not knowing where he was going. By faith he lived as an alien in the land of promise, as in a foreign land, dwelling in tents with Isaac and Jacob, fellow*

heirs of the same promise; for he was looking for the city
which has foundations, whose architect and builder is
God. (Hebrews 11:8-10)

Abraham received the call of God and obeyed Him, not knowing where he was going. God led him one step at a time and in his
obedience, Abraham kept on stepping. His obedience to the faith
was governed by his trust in God and not in his ability to see what
was ahead. We as believers do not know what tomorrow brings, but
while we are waiting for that day to come we are called to obey God
by faith, in the present. It is obedience to the faith on a daily basis
that produces the fruit of righteousness in the believer's life.

The Trust of Faith

The trust of faith is stressed in the life of Sarah.

By faith even Sarah herself received ability to conceive,
even beyond the proper time of life, since she considered
Him faithful who had promised. Therefore there was born
even of one man, and him as good as dead at that, as
many descendants AS THE STARS OF HEAVEN IN
NUMBER, AND INNUMERABLE AS THE SAND
WHICH IS BY THE SEASHORE. (Hebrews 11:11-12)

Even though Sarah's circumstances were beyond her control,
she trusted in the faithfulness of God to fulfill His promises. Her
faith recognized the fact that God's promises superseded anything that appeared impossible from her viewpoint.

The believer's faith to trust God is rooted in the divine promises of His Word and not the nature of his circumstances, as ideal
or impossible, as they may seem. Faith always believes against the
impossible when God has guaranteed His promises to His people.

The Future Reward of Faith

In verses 13-16, our attention is drawn to the *future reward of faith.*

> *All these died in faith, without receiving the promises,*
> *but having seen them and having welcomed them from a*
> *distance, and having confessed that they were strangers*
> *and exiles on the earth. For those who say such things*
> *make it clear that they are seeking a country of their*
> *own. And indeed if they had been thinking of that coun-*
> *try from which they went out, they would have had*
> *opportunity to return. But as it is, they desire a better*
> *country, that is, a heavenly one. Therefore God is not*
> *ashamed to be called their God; for He has prepared a*
> *city for them.* (Hebrews 11:13-16)

Great men of faith know that the ultimate reward for trusting God is beyond this life. They are prepared to lose everything in this life knowing the true treasures are awaiting them in heaven. Men who possess this kind of faith are consumed with one thing, to do the will of the Father on earth. Verse 16 should not go unnoticed, *"God is not ashamed to be called their God."* The magnitude of this statement speaks volumes to the believer. The awesome God of heaven is not ashamed to identify with believers in Christ. In a world that considers the believer unworthy, an individual's faith is commendable before the Father. What better place to be than to have God in our corner, even if the world is against us? (cf. Romans 8:31). The ultimate reward of faith is always in the future; therefore, we should patiently wait for the day when God will reward us generously for all eternity.

The Test of Faith

In verses 17-19, the *test of faith* is expressed in the relationship of Abraham and his son, Isaac.

> *By faith Abraham, when he was tested, offered up Isaac,*
> *and he who had received the promises was offering up his*
> *only begotten son; it was he to whom it was said, "IN*
> *ISAAC YOUR DESCENDANTS SHALL BE CALLED."*
> *He considered that God is able to raise people even from*
> *the dead, from which he also received him back as a type.*
> (Hebrews 11:17-19)

Abraham was willing to sacrifice the most precious treasure in his life, his son, in order to follow the will of God. This event was the test of Abraham's faith. It proved he was ready to follow God no matter what the Father commanded him to do. He was prepared to serve God with a complete disregard for his own interest.

This episode in the life of Abraham, the testing of his faith, is repeated in different ways in the personal lives of all of us. Although the circumstances may be different, there will come a place and time when God will test the sincerity of faith in His children. God will test our hearts to see if we are willing to give up the most precious items in this life that hinder us from making Him first in our lives. God's intent is not to disqualify us, but to edify the believer who is given the opportunity to authenticate his love for God. A faith that has been tested in this manner builds confidence in the believer, assuring that his heart belongs fully to God.

The Inheritance of Faith

In verses 20-22, the *inheritance of faith* is portrayed in the life of the patriarchs.

*By faith Isaac blessed Jacob and Esau, even regarding
things to come. By faith Jacob, as he was dying, blessed
each of the sons of Joseph, and worshiped, leaning on the
top of his staff. By faith Joseph, when he was dying, made
mention of the exodus of the sons of Israel, and gave orders
concerning his bones.* (Hebrews 11:20-22)

The personal faith of these men had an impact upon future
generations. Even as they were dying, their words testified to
where their hearts were. They instructed their family members to
pursue the things that were of God. The death of a believer is not
the end of one's witness for God. His faith lives in the hearts of
his descendants. How many times do we hear how a grandparent,
who went to be with the Lord, had a tremendous impact on a
family member in leading him or her to salvation? In the same
way, if God tarries, we are called to leave an impact upon future
generations for the gospel message after we are gone.

The Direction, Courage, and Depth of Faith

In the life of Moses three aspects of faith are displayed.

*By faith Moses, when he was born, was hidden for three
months by his parents, because they saw he was a beautiful child; and they were not afraid of the king's edict. By
faith Moses, when he had grown up, refused to be called
the son of Pharaoh's daughter, choosing rather to endure
ill-treatment with the people of God than to enjoy the
passing pleasures of sin, considering the reproach of
Christ greater riches than the treasures of Egypt; for he
was looking to the reward. By faith he left Egypt, not fear-
ing the wrath of the king; for he endured, as seeing Him
who is unseen. By faith he kept the Passover and the*

sprinkling of the blood, so that he who destroyed the first-born would not touch them. By faith they passed through the Red Sea as though they were passing through dry land; and the Egyptians, when they attempted it, were drowned. (Hebrews 11:23-29)

The first aspect is *the direction of faith*. Moses, knowing that he was born a Hebrew, refused to identify with his Egyptian upbringing. He separated himself from Pharaoh's family and chose to identify with his ill-treated countrymen. He considered the riches of Egypt to be petty in comparison to the eternal treasures that come with faith in God. True faith directs the believer towards right decisions.

Second, the *courage of faith* is displayed throughout the life of Moses. His decisions revealed a fearless personality. It is this courage in faith that helped him stand alone as an underdog against the Egyptians and to witness the awesomeness of God in delivering the Jewish people. True faith expresses itself in a courageous way.

Third, from the life of Moses, we also witness the *depth of faith*. His belief in God did not stop when he was confronted with an impossible situation. When we have the assurance of God's Word, true faith is not just surface deep, but our belief emanates from the innermost part of our being. The depth of faith gives us solid footing to stand firm for the truth.

The Victory of Faith

In verse 30, the **victory of faith** is portrayed at the walls of Jericho.

By faith the walls of Jericho fell down after they had been encircled for seven days. (Hebrews 11:30)

The walls of Jericho represent the walls of difficulty. No matter how bad or impossible a given situation might appear, a solid faith in God will penetrate the walls of difficulty. God will remove these obstacles when we choose to trust in Him.

The Impartiality of Faith

In verse 31, the practice of faith by Rahab shows the *impartiality of faith.*

By faith Rahab the harlot did not perish along with those who were disobedient, after she had welcomed the spies in peace. (Hebrews 11:31)

Rahab was a harlot, but this did not stop her ability to believe in the truth of God. Her lifestyle is not what is being endorsed in this verse, but rather the fact that she feared the God of Israel. The implication of this text shows that no matter what one's background may be, God is concerned about a heart that is willing to believe in Him and turns away from ungodly practices. Saving faith is what erases the past and ushers in the new life we have in Jesus Christ. The impartiality of faith is what makes it possible for the worst of sinners, who put their faith in Jesus Christ, to participate in the eternal blessings of God. The believer can rejoice that God has accepted him just the way he is when he comes into the family of God through faith. Therefore, we should not be saddled down by our past sins, since God, through faith, has erased them for all eternity.

The Great Displays of Faith

The remainder of the chapter records the great displays of faith given to us throughout the Old Testament.

And what more shall I say? For time will fail me if I tell of
Gideon, Barak, Samson, Jephthah, of David and Samuel
and the prophets, who by faith conquered kingdoms, per-
formed acts of righteousness, obtained promises, shut the
mouths of lions, quenched the power of fire, escaped the
edge of the sword, from weakness were made strong,
became mighty in war, put foreign armies to flight.
Women received back their dead by resurrection; and oth-
ers were tortured, not accepting their release, so that they
might obtain a better resurrection; and others experienced
mockings and scourgings, yes, also chains and imprison-
ment. They were stoned, they were sawn in two, they were
tempted, they were put to death with the sword; they
went about in sheepskins, in goatskins, being destitute,
afflicted, ill-treated (men of whom the world was not
worthy), wandering in deserts and mountains and caves
and holes in the ground. And all these, having gained
approval through their faith, did not receive what was
promised, because God had provided something better for
us, so that apart from us they would not be made perfect.
(Hebrews 11:32-40)

These were men and women who were considered unworthy by the standard of the world (cf. Verse 38). Their lives were
looked upon as unimportant and they passed into history
unnoticed by man. No one considered writing about them or
recording any of their deeds accomplished through their acts of
faith. However, in contrast, as insignificant as they were to man,
their lives were like a beacon light before the throne of God.
Their accomplishments through faith did not go unnoticed
before their Father in heaven. God has documented every act of
faith that was prompted by their love for Him. They never

received the promises of God on earth, but they fully understood that their rewards were waiting for them in heaven for all eternity.

We are encouraged by the author of Hebrews to reflect upon these great men and women who have gone before us.

> *Therefore, since we are surrounded by such a great cloud of witnesses, let us throw off everything that hinders and the sin that so easily entangles, and let us run with perseverance the race marked out for us.* (Hebrews 12:1 NIV)

In following their example, the author admonishes the believers to throw off anything that would slow their progress or hinder them from running the race for God. The sin in this passage is the sin of unbelief that fails to trust in the finished work of Jesus Christ. The most unnecessary baggage in the believer's life is unbelief. Lack of trust is what hinders the believer from persevering and walking in the abundant life he has in Jesus Christ. Faith is the means by which we reduce the effects of unbelief and accept the testimony of God's Word. God has called us to stand firm in the faith, in our Christian walk.

THE AUTHOR OF OUR FAITH

As God's people, we are to guard against unbelief by cultivating our relationship with God on a daily basis, fixing our eyes on the author of our faith, Jesus Christ.

> *Let us fix our eyes on Jesus, the author and perfecter of our faith, who for the joy set before him endured the cross, scorning its shame, and sat down at the right hand of the*

throne of God. Consider him who endured such opposition from sinful men, so that you will not grow weary and lose heart. (Hebrews 12:2-3 NIV)

As we look to Jesus Christ, the focus and strength of our faith, we will grow in our trust in God with the assurance and confidence that comes from a faith-filled life. The weariness and discouragement of our circumstances will be replaced with the joy and peace that God's people experience when they believe wholeheartedly in Him. There is no mountain or obstacle the believer cannot overcome. The church saint, who trusts in God with all his heart, will never be defeated in his Christian walk. His accomplishments for the kingdom of God will go far beyond his own imagination.

Now to Him who is able to do far more abundantly beyond all that we ask or think, according to the power that works within us, to Him be the glory in the church and in Christ Jesus to all generations forever and ever. Amen. (Ephesians 3:20-21)

Chapter Twelve

MAKING A DIFFERENCE

Therefore, if anyone is in Christ, he is a new creation; the old has gone, the new has come! All this is from God, who reconciled us to himself through Christ and gave us the ministry of reconciliation: that God was reconciling the world to himself in Christ, not counting men's sins against them. And he has committed to us the message of reconciliation. **We are therefore Christ's ambassadors, as though God were making his appeal through us.** *We implore you on Christ's behalf: Be reconciled to God. God made him who had no sin to be sin for us, so that in him we might become the righteousness of God.* (2 Corinthians 5:17-21, emphasis added NIV)

AMBASSADORS OF GOD

Believers are the ambassadors of God through whom He is making His appeal to the world in revealing the truth of Jesus Christ. God is not using the powerful angels of heaven or the unbelieving rich and famous of this world to carry forth His truth, but sinners who have turned to Him in repentance. We are His instruments and vessels, making a difference in a world that has forgotten the goodness of God. If this is so, how much do we need to walk according to the purpose of our calling?

GUARDING AGAINST COMPLACENCY

In order to be an effective ambassador, the church saint needs to maintain his spiritual fervor. He must continue to mature and live a Spirit-filled life throughout his Christian walk. One of the most devastating traits that plagues believers is complacency. It is not as easy to detect as a sin that is a direct violation of God's Word. It has gone undetected in many individuals and congregations throughout the generations of the church. Regrettably, this behavior is more harmful and damaging than obvious sins, which can be policed by the congregation. Perhaps this is the reason it has been detrimental to the spiritual well-being of the believer and the church as a whole. The believer needs to constantly guard against this damaging attitude in serving God. Since this sin has found a way to hide itself, it demands our attention. The character and essence of complacency can be described in this way: it is a failure to go on to maturity in the Christian life. It is finding satisfaction in our spiritual walk without any desire to grow in the grace of God. It is failing to let God stretch us to the limit in order to be effective instruments for Him. The believer feels he has arrived and his love for God has grown cold. This is a treacherous place for the child of God. It is interesting to note what Webster's dictionary says about complacency:

Self satisfaction accompanied by unawareness of actual dangers or deficiencies.

This definition couldn't be any closer to the truth when relating it to a complacent believer. The believer not only is failing to uphold his obligation to God when he is complacent, but is totally clueless of his spiritual deficiency.

This concealed fault in the believer and the church as a whole needs to be corrected. Many Christians start their walk on fire with every intention of serving God wholeheartedly, but before long stagnation infiltrates the heart and mind of the believer. They become spectators to the faith instead of *warriors for God* who penetrate the darkness of Satan's dominion on earth.

STANDING FIRM (MAINTAINING SPIRITUAL INTENSITY)

How does the church maintain the spiritual intensity that is required to experience the fullness of our calling in Christ? How do we continue to live a Spirit-filled life for God that will make a difference for the gospel of Jesus Christ? There is one phrase in the Scriptures that is repeated throughout the epistles: *Stand firm*. The believer needs to *stand firm* in the Lord.

> *Therefore, my dear brothers, stand firm. Let nothing move you. Always give yourselves fully to the work of the Lord, because you know that your labor in the Lord is not in vain.* (1 Corinthians 15:58 NIV)

God wants our feet so anchored in the truth that nothing in this world can uproot our beliefs. We are to be totally consumed in the Lord's business—growing and maturing in our faith in order to become unmovable by the trials and struggles of life. In order to stand firm, there should be a three-dimensional outlook by which the believer lives. These dimensions have a past, present, and future perspective. All three are alluded to in the Apostle Paul's letter to the Philippians.

Brethren, I do not regard myself as having laid hold of it yet; but one thing I do: **forgetting what lies behind** *and* **reaching forward to what lies ahead,** *I press on toward the goal for the prize of the upward call of God in Christ Jesus. Let us therefore, as many as are perfect, have this attitude; and if in anything you have a different attitude, God will reveal that also to you; however,* **let us keep living by that same standard to which we have attained.**
(Philippians 3:13-16, emphasis added)

(1) Past perspective: Forget what lies behind.
(2) Future perspective: Reach forward to what lies ahead.
(3) Present perspective: Live up to the standard to which we have attained.

Paul, in this passage, is contrasting the Law with the grace of God in Christ. The fullness of the believer's walk comes when his life is hidden in Christ, not by returning to the old standard. In verse 13, we see the past and future perspective to standing firm in the faith. Paul says to *forget what lies behind* and *reach forward to what lies ahead*. In reality he is saying, in this context, to forget the old standard of righteousness under the Law and press on to the hope the believer has in Christ. These believers are to look to the new life they have in Christ, pursuing the hope of eternal life. This future perspective of hope is what purifies the believer in his daily walk.

And everyone who has this hope fixed on Him purifies himself, just as He is pure. (1 John 3:3)

The believers, who adjust to Paul's admonishment, will continue in a conduct that is meaningful and edifying to their personal walk with God. If they fail to adhere to Paul's words, they will find themselves stalled in their Christian walk by reverting to the old manner of life.

The application is this: are we living in the past, in which certain fruitless practices still exist in our lives that are detrimental to our present walk with God? Have we stalled our forward progress because we are failing to allow the Holy Spirit to lead and guide us in the things that are eternal? Are we failing to cultivate the hope we have in Jesus Christ, back-pedaling into a hopeless past? Our focus needs to be on eternal things that are meaningful and true. Can we take on the same attitude Paul had in wanting to know Christ and forgetting the things that lie behind?

> *But whatever was to my profit I now consider loss for the sake of Christ. What is more, I consider everything a loss compared to the surpassing greatness of knowing Christ Jesus my Lord, for whose sake I have lost all things. I consider them rubbish, that I may gain Christ and be found in him, not having a righteousness of my own that comes from the law, but that which is through faith in Christ— the righteousness that comes from God and is by faith. I* **want to know Christ** *and the power of his resurrection and the fellowship of sharing in his sufferings, becoming like him in his death, and so, somehow, to attain to the resurrection from the dead.* (Philippians 3:7-11 NIV, emphasis added)

Paul in this passage is driven by his desire to know Jesus Christ who dwells in him. He is not about to allow anything to interfere or hinder his pursuit of righteousness in knowing Christ in all His fullness. His hope in this life is looking forward to what lies ahead. *"I press on towards the goal for the prize of the upward call of God in Christ Jesus"* (Philippians 3:14). This is the essence of a practicing Christian, living for Jesus Christ.

> *For the love of Christ controls us, having concluded this, that one died for all, therefore all died; and He died for all, so that they who live might no longer live for themselves, but for Him who died and rose again on their behalf.* (2 Corinthians 5:14-15)

It is not about practicing religion with prescribed rites, but a personal relationship with Jesus Christ in which one is doing everything possible through the grace of God to be more like Him. If one's Christianity is based upon this premise for maturity, then he will lay a solid foundation for remaining unmovable in his faith in Jesus Christ.

The third dimension for standing firm is to live up to the standard we have attained in our spiritual walk. *"Let us keep living by that same standard to which we have attained"* (Philippians 3:16). As we continue to grow, we should not allow ourselves to grow lax or fall back in areas of our lives that we have already matured in. The believer can prevent this by continuing to grow in the grace of God. Our mindset should always seek fulfillment in our faith but never be satisfied with where we are in our maturity. This is the admonishment of Peter in encouraging the believer to persevere in the faith.

> *For this very reason, make every effort to add to your faith goodness; and to goodness, knowledge; and to knowledge, self-control; and to self-control, perseverance; and to perseverance, godliness; and to godliness, brotherly kindness; and to brotherly kindness, love. For if you possess these qualities in increasing measure,* **they will keep you from being**

ineffective and unproductive *in your knowledge of our Lord Jesus Christ. But if anyone does not have them, he is nearsighted and blind, and has forgotten that he has been cleansed from his past sins. Therefore, my brothers, be all the more eager to make your calling and election sure. For if you do these things, you will never fall, and you will receive a rich welcome into the eternal kingdom of our Lord and Savior Jesus Christ.* (2 Peter 1:5-11, emphasis added NIV)

Remember, there is only one speed in the Christian walk: full speed ahead. Apart from this pace we run the risk of becoming ineffective and unproductive vessels. It has been said that if a shark stops moving, he will end up drowning. He is an eating machine that is constantly on the prowl. This serves as a good illustration of the believer, who in the same manner, must persistently move forward in his faith. If he becomes complacent he will end up falling behind, failing in his walk for God. This was what Jesus Christ was alluding to when He spoke about the believing subjects of God's kingdom.

As they were going along the road, someone said to Him, "I will follow You wherever You go." And Jesus said to him, "The foxes have holes and the birds of the air have nests, but the Son of Man has nowhere to lay His head." And He said to another, "Follow Me." But he said, "Lord, permit me first to go and bury my father." But He said to him, "Allow the dead to bury their own dead; but as for you, go and proclaim everywhere the kingdom of God." Another also said, "I will follow You, Lord; but first permit me to say good-bye to those at home." But Jesus said to him, **"No one, after putting his hand to the plow and looking back, is fit for the kingdom of God."** (Luke 9:57-62, emphasis added)

The excuses in this passage revealed that the hearers were not up to the task of following Christ. They were holding on to the things of this world too tightly, preventing them from following Christ with all their hearts. It was their hearts that stopped them and not their circumstances. Remember, God has equipped us with everything necessary to persevere spiritually or physically. The enemy Satan is constantly attempting to blind us from this reality. He is looking to devour someone and shatter his or her confidence and faith in God.

Be of sober spirit, be on the alert. Your adversary, the devil, prowls around like a roaring lion, seeking someone to devour. (1 Peter 5:8)

If Satan is successful in his relentless attacks, the believer becomes a useless vessel for God. The believer needs to be of sober spirit and alert, fighting back with the Word of God instead of succumbing to the lies of Satan. The Scriptures remind us every day of our new relationship in Jesus Christ and the victory we have in Him.

When Satan tempted Jesus in the wilderness, Christ fought back with the Word of God. We can do no better than to fight back with the Bible and proclaim the victory that we all have in Christ. There is no reason why any of us should fall short of our obligation to our calling. God will always provide the grace and mercy we need. If we are falling short of our purpose, it is we who need to change and not the Father. Trust God and walk in the fullness of our great salvation in Christ Jesus.

This life is a mist that quickly vanishes compared to eternity (cf. James 4:14). We need to make the most of our opportunities and time while here on earth. Our lives need to be spent in doing the Lord's will. We have been delivered from the kingdom of darkness into the kingdom of light; therefore, let us walk in our new life in Christ.

> *For you were once darkness, but now you are light in the*
> *Lord. Live as children of light (for the fruit of the light*
> *consists in all goodness, righteousness and truth) and find*
> *out what pleases the Lord. Have nothing to do with the*
> *fruitless deeds of darkness, but rather expose them. For it is*
> *shameful even to mention what the disobedient do in*
> *secret. But everything exposed by the light becomes visible,*
> *for it is light that makes everything visible. This is why it is*
> *said: "Wake up, O sleeper, rise from the dead, and Christ*
> *will shine on you." Be very careful, then, how you live—*
> *not as unwise but as wise, making the most of every*
> *opportunity, because the days are evil. Therefore do not be*
> *foolish, but understand what the Lord's will is. Do not get*
> *drunk on wine, which leads to debauchery. Instead, be*
> *filled with the Spirit. Speak to one another with psalms,*
> *hymns and spiritual songs. Sing and make music in your*
> *heart to the Lord, always giving thanks to God the Father*
> *for everything, in the name of our Lord Jesus Christ.*
> (Ephesians 5:8-20 NIV)

PICKING UP OUR CROSS

One final thought: Most everything this world promotes opposes the teaching of Jesus Christ and what He stands for. Jesus told His disciples in the gospels to pick up their cross. What exactly did He mean? In Roman times, crucifixion on the cross identified the person as a criminal of the state. It was the Roman government's way of saying to the people that the one who was crucified was wrong and they were right in carrying out the punishment. As we pick up our own cross, we are identifying with the rejection of Jesus Christ by the world (cf. John 15:18-21). By identifying with this rejection, we are identifying with the truth of Christ. In so doing, we are called to turn the tables and tell the world they are wrong and that Jesus Christ is right. This is a huge mountain to climb, but the practice of faith will help us stand our ground against those who oppose the truth of Jesus Christ.

When David fought Goliath, he appeared to be at a tremendous disadvantage. He overcame this apparent insurmountable obstacle by trusting in God. His faith took him beyond his fears into a place where he proclaimed the greatness of God.

> *Then David said to the Philistine, "You come to me with a sword, a spear, and a javelin, but I come to you in the name of the LORD of hosts, the God of the armies of Israel, whom you have taunted."* (1 Samuel 17:45)

He was fully aware that Goliath was the underdog, since he was coming up against the God of Israel. David knew that God blesses His servants who put their faith in Him. In the same way, there are many *Goliaths* the believer will face in this lifetime, but for those who have trusted wholeheartedly in God, these obstacles will fall by the wayside.

As mentioned in chapter 1 and now reiterated, this book testifies to the storehouse of riches that God has made available to us in our heavenly calling. God is speaking to His servants today to uphold their purpose as Christians, completing the task of testifying to the truth of Jesus Christ. Consider the words of the Apostle Paul in his determination to complete his task.

> *And now, compelled by the Spirit, I am going to Jerusalem, not knowing what will happen to me there. I only know*

that in every city the Holy Spirit warns me that prison and hardships are facing me. However, I consider my life worth nothing to me, if only I may finish the race and complete the task the Lord Jesus has given me—the task of testifying to the gospel of God's grace. (Acts 20:22-24 NIV)

The time is now, as God's ambassadors, to stand firm for Christ and the truth. The time is now to reach in to all our resources the Father has equipped us with, and make a difference in this world for God. We are the *light of the world* that penetrates the darkness that has come over people's hearts. We are the *salt of the earth* that preserves truth and allows the lost to taste the goodness of God in all His grace and mercy. Our obligation is to make an impact for the gospel of Jesus Christ. It takes a mature Christian who knows how to stand his ground against the schemes of the enemy to complete this mission.

We are God's workmanship created in Christ Jesus to produce the fruit of righteousness; therefore, the Father in heaven is shaping and molding us into the wonderful image of Jesus Christ. Rejoice my brothers and sisters in God's love and the plans that He has for all of us.

I pray that the eyes of your heart may be enlightened, so that you will know what is the hope of His calling, what are the riches of the glory of His inheritance in the saints, and what is the surpassing greatness of His power toward us who believe. (Ephesians 1:18-19a)

AMEN!

God's Workmanship Under Grace
Order Form

E-mail orders: ccbctom@aol.com

Please send *God's Workmanship Under Grace* **to:**

Name: _____

Address: _____

City: _____ State: _____

Zip: _____ Telephone: (_____) _____

Book Price: $13.95

Shipping: $3.00 for the first book and $1.00 for each additional book to cover shipping and handling within US, Canada, and Mexico. International orders add $6.00 for the first book and $2.00 for each additional book.

Or order from:
ACW Press
1200 HWY 231 South #273
Ozark, AL 36360

(800) 931-BOOK

or contact your local bookstore